**What was Indiana Jones doing
in Hawaii in October 1914?**

Indiana Jones is that world-famous, whip-cracking hero you know from the movies...

But was he *always* cool and fearless in the face of danger? Did he *always* get mixed up in hair-raising, heart-stopping escapades?

Yes!

Read all about Indy as a kid. Watch him as he battles both the fury of an erupting volcano and the wrath of a German officer who wants him dead. Get ready for some edge-of-your-seat excitement!

YOUNG INDIANA JONES BOOKS
(original novels)

Young Indiana Jones and the...
1. Plantation Treasure
2. Tomb of Terror
3. Circle of Death
4. Secret City
5. Princess of Peril
6. Gypsy Revenge
7. Ghostly Riders
8. Curse of the Ruby Cross
9. Titanic Adventure
10. Lost Gold of Durango
11. Face of the Dragon
12. Journey to the Underworld
13. Mountain of Fire
14. Pirates' Loot

THE YOUNG INDIANA JONES CHRONICLES
(novels based on the television series)

TV-1. The Mummy's Curse
TV-2. Field of Death
TV-3. Safari Sleuth
TV-4. The Secret Peace
TV-5. Trek of Doom
TV-6. Revolution!
TV-7. Race to Danger
TV-8. Prisoner of War

YOUNG INDIANA JONES™
and the
MOUNTAIN OF FIRE

By William McCay

Bullseye Books

Random House 🏠 New York

A BULLSEYE BOOK PUBLISHED BY RANDOM HOUSE, INC.

Copyright © 1994 by Lucasfilm Ltd. (LFL)

All rights reserved under International and Pan-American Copyright Conventions. Published in the United States by Random House, Inc., New York, and simultaneously in Canada by Random House of Canada Limited, Toronto.

Young Indy novels are conceived and produced by Random House, Inc., in conjunction with Lucasfilm Ltd.

Library of Congress Cataloging-in-Publication Data:
McCay, William.
Young Indiana Jones and the mountain of fire / by William McCay.
  p. cm. — (Young Indiana Jones books ; #13)
SUMMARY: While visiting Hawaii in the early days of World War One, Indy and his friend Lizzie Ravenall uncover a plot to sabotage British shipping in the Pacific.
ISBN 0-679-86384-2 (pbk.)
1. World War, 1914–1918—Juvenile Fiction. [1. World War, 1914–1918—Fiction. 2. Adventure and adventurers—Fiction. 3. Hawaii—Fiction.]
I. Title. II. Series.
PZ7.M4784136Yom 1994 [Fic]—dc20 93-46118

Manufactured in the United States of America 10 9 8 7 6 5 4 3 2 1

TM & © 1994 Lucasfilm Ltd. (LFL). All rights reserved.

Chapter 1

The sun looked like a huge, bloodshot eyeball sinking into the Pacific Ocean. Young Indiana Jones stared back from the bow of the *China Maid*. The other passengers were gathering in the steamship's stern to hear Mrs. Hagedorn give an after-dinner recital.

Indy had other concerns. Tonight, he planned to go somewhere he'd never been before. All he had to do was wait—until everyone went to sleep.

Great events had taken place in this autumn of 1914. Vast armies marched as Germany invaded Belgium. French and British forces had fought desperately to keep the Germans out of Paris. When Indy and his father had boarded this ship in the beginning of October, the two sides were dug in across Europe. But so much could have happened in the time since the *China Maid* left San Francisco! The ship had no wireless receiver. So there was no news.

The singing recital finally ended, and Indy headed back to the other passengers. It was a short enough walk. The *China Maid* was less than four hundred feet long and barely sixty feet wide. And from the wheelhouse where the sailors steered the ship, to the engine room where sweaty men heaved coal into the throbbing steam engines, Indy had seen every foot.

He smiled in the growing darkness as he joined his father. Pretty soon everyone would be asleep. Everyone but Indy.

Professor Henry Jones led the way to their cabin, then stopped and glanced over his glasses. "Have you done today's reading, Junior?"

Indy frowned. Since he was missing school during their travels, his college-professor father was tutoring him. This question sounded like the start of a pop quiz.

"Who unified the Hawaiian Islands in 1793?" asked the Professor once they were back in their cabin. Since they had a stopover in the Hawaiian Islands on the way to China, Indy was learning about Hawaiian language and history.

"King Kamehameha conquered almost all of the Hawaiian Islands by 1793," Indy answered.

"And the last Hawaiian monarch?"

"Lily of Kilanney," Indy said.

"Henry!" Professor Jones shook his head. "Where did you learn that?"

"That's how the sailors on board pronounce it," said Indy.

"The queen's name is Liliuokalani." Indy's father pronounced each syllable distinctly: lil-ee-oo-ka-*la*-nee. "Her rank deserves respect, even if she was deposed in 1893.

"When did the Hawaiian Islands become an American territory?"

"In 1898," Indy answered promptly.

"Wrong!" The professor pounced. "The correct date is 1900."

Indy thought hard. "Hawaii became a territory in 1900," he said brightly. "But the annexation passed Congress in 1898."

Professor Jones cleared his throat. "Ah. Of course. An act of Congress. Humph."

Indy had to hide a grin. The truth was, his father was more comfortable with the doings of kings and emperors of long ago. Professor Jones specialized in the literature of the Middle Ages. Indy suspected that his father thought Columbus had somehow spoiled things by sailing off to the New World.

"Honolulu is supposed to be quite some place," Indy said. "It's the only American city that has a royal palace, even if Queen Liliuokalani *was* deposed."

Professor Jones smiled at that thought. Then he stretched and gave a big yawn. "I think that will be all for the evening," he said. "Something about this sea air..."

Indy nodded. Once again he hid a smile. Things were going just as he'd hoped. Dad would fall asleep now, and he slept like a log on ocean voyages.

Professor Jones turned out the lights, and very soon he was snoring to beat the band.

Indy slid out from under the covers and groped in the darkness until he found his pants. Then he crept to the door. He didn't bother bringing his shoes along. Where he planned to go, he wouldn't need them.

Quietly, Indy opened the door and stepped out onto the deck. The portholes of the passenger cabins were all dark.

Yes, he thought. Tonight was the night.

The *China Maid* had been built in 1899. Like Indy, it was fifteen years old. Back then, trading ships were still being built with masts.

Indy's dad had put up with most of Indy's exploring on the ship. But there was one place he had forbidden him to go.

"I don't want to see you up on those masts, Henry," he'd said.

That was why Indy was going climbing at night. Dad was asleep. He *wouldn't* see Indy on the masts.

Indy reached up to the ratline, a rope ladder, and began to climb. Up he went—ten feet, then another ten, aiming for the crow's nest about halfway up the mast.

At this point, Indy realized that the nest

was a lot higher up than he had thought. He had a good fifty feet left to go.

Nor had he expected the sway. Down on deck, the ship rolled slightly with the waves. But up here, the mast swung back and forth by several feet. The higher Indy went, the more the mast rocked.

Indy gritted his teeth and kept climbing. By the time he'd almost reached the crow's nest, he felt like he was on a carnival ride. His fingers clung to the rope ladder. Even his toes curled around it.

Now Indy realized that he didn't have to worry about falling to the deck if he lost his grip. The way the mast was swinging, he'd probably be thrown out into the sea.

Maybe I don't need to climb *all* the way, Indy told himself.

He was amazed at how much farther he could see from up here. The moon was up, and it cast a silver lane across the sea. And deep in the water, tiny creatures of some kind were glowing greenish-blue. Indy finally risked a glance downward. The deck looked very small.

Indy squinted. A small craft had pulled

up beside the *China Maid*. Even as Indy watched, a shadowy figure swung over the *China Maid*'s rail. Stealthily, the form headed for the middle of the ship, where the smokestack rose.

Who could it be? A pirate? Indy was about to yell a challenge. But instead he closed his mouth so hard his teeth clicked. If he made a ruckus, the captain and crew would come out. So would the passengers. And Indy's father would see him in the one place he didn't want to see him.

I'll watch for a few more seconds, Indy decided. If anything bad starts happening, I can always yell then.

The mystery boarder prowled around the smokestack and disappeared into the shadows. A moment later, the strange visitor went back to the rail, swung down a line, and landed in the little boat. A second later, the dinghy was drifting away.

What's going on? Indy wondered. There's nothing around there to steal. He began climbing down. By the time he reached the deck, the small craft had vanished into the night. Straining his ears, Indy thought he could hear the faint puttering of an engine in the distance.

With a shrug, Indy headed over to the smokestack. The big funnel rose at least three times his height. And as he began walking around it, Indy caught a muted ticking sound. It came from the shadows where the moonlight didn't reach.

Indy almost missed what he was searching for, but then his foot hit something. He dropped to one knee and peered into the darkness. Dim outlines became visible. There seemed to be some sort of clock—that was where the ticking came from. Indy saw wires, and an indistinct bundle.

He looked closer and went pale There before him was a bundle of waxy sticks—dynamite.

"Holy crow!" Indy whispered. His throat was tight. "I've stumbled across a time bomb!"

Chapter 2

Indy tiptoed back from the bomb as if it were a fierce beast he didn't want to awaken. The adventure magazines he loved to read always had the villains building bombs—they called them "infernal devices."

Peering into the shadows, Indy wished the authors of those stories had spent a bit more time explaining how those infernal devices worked. More to the point, it would be nice to know how to take them apart.

Indy looked more closely at the deadly little package. He traced the wires from the clock to some gadget hidden among the dynamite sticks. His first thought was to toss the whole thing overboard.

But did he dare jostle it? Maybe not. Seconds were ticking away, and he had no way of knowing when the bomb was set to go off. Indy took a deep breath and began yelling for help.

The first mate, who was the officer on watch, came stumbling from the wheelhouse. He rubbed his eyes and tucked in his shirt. At first he was annoyed that his sleep had been interrupted. Then he saw the bomb—and he, too, went pale.

"I know a little about electricity," he said. He dropped to his knees. Carefully, he shifted the bomb out into the moonlight. "Maybe I can figure out where these wires go."

By now the captain, as well as several passengers, had been awakened. The captain was louder than the mate in his complaints. And he was much slower to understand. As the captain asked questions, Indy could smell whisky fumes on his breath. But the more the captain understood what was going on, the more sober he became.

"This one here," the first mate said. He separated out one wire. "I think."

Indy closed his eyes as the man yanked

on the wire. When there was no explosion, he opened his eyes to see the mate holding the clock in one hand and the dynamite in the other.

Then the captain began asking Indy more questions. "You say someone boarded the ship?" he demanded. "Why didn't you raise the alarm?"

"I...uh...I didn't..." Indy stumbled over his words. He hadn't thought ahead to come up with a story to cover himself. And as he saw the nightshirt-clad figure of his father, Indy knew he was in trouble.

"Yes, Junior," Professor Jones said. "Why didn't you give any warning? What were you doing out on deck in the first place?"

"I, um, wasn't exactly *on* the deck." Indy wished he weren't on the deck right now. Maybe the North Pole would be a better place to be. From the look on his father's face, things were getting pretty cold anyway.

"You were climbing the masts?" The professor's voice rose. "How can you explain that, after I forbade you?"

"Actually, you said you didn't want to *see me* climbing the masts," Indy said.

"Exactly!" Professor Jones was about to yell some more. But he stopped. "Ah," he said. "You decided to take me literally."

Indy thought of the "Unclear!" his father had scribbled over his last composition. He just nodded.

"Such an interest in precision in the English language should be rewarded," Professor Jones growled. "I'll assign some additional essays. We can discuss them privately, and leave the captain to his investigation."

"What investigation?" the captain asked. He rubbed his whiskery face. "We've got a bomb here, but whoever left it got away."

The first mate still held the deactivated bomb gingerly, half in one hand, half in the other. "It must have something to do with the war," he said. "Maybe the Germans came and planted a bomb on us. I hear they've got these boats that go underwater— submarines."

"A submarine—out here?" The captain turned scornful eyes on his second in command. "I *might* be able to believe that—if you could tell me why the Germans would want to sink an old tub like this."

Boy, Indy thought, he sure sounds proud of his ship.

"Light off the starboard bow!" the helmsman suddenly called out.

"That's the lighthouse at Makapuu Point," the captain said. "We're right off the island of Oahu."

Maybe he wasn't proud of his ship, but the captain took good care of it. He turned to the wheelhouse. "Signal the engine room," he called up. "Full stop until daybreak. There are reefs in these waters, and I've never been through here before."

One of the awakened passengers spoke up. "I thought your ship always refueled at Hawaii."

"But we're on a new route, and Hawaii is a big place," the captain said. "These islands stretch a good fifteen hundred miles. That's like the distance from Boston to New Orleans."

"That far?" the passenger said.

The captain nodded. "The *China Maid* usually takes on fresh coal at Hilo, on the big island of Hawaii. That's two hundred and twenty-five miles to the southeast of us.

But on that route, our port of call is Shanghai, which is farther south on the China coast."

That was as much as Indy heard while his father was marching him back to their cabin. Anything more on deck was shut out by the slamming of the cabin door.

When Indy got up the next morning, the *China Maid* had already begun chugging on. As he arrived on deck, the ship steamed through the mouth of Honolulu harbor.

"Too bad we're not on a Matson Line ship," Sergeant Warrick, a soldier traveling on board, told him. "They're the topflight steamers to Hawaii. When one of them arrives, the whole waterfront turns out."

The old soldier grinned. "Ship day, they call it. I remember back in '98, when we passed through on our way to the Philippines. These pretty *wahines*—those are young girls, lad—were all lined up to greet us. Each soldier got a *lei*."

"That's a flower necklace, right?" Indy asked.

"Right," the sergeant said. "There was a band playing, and we marched to the camp out there on that point jutting into the water." He pointed to the huge rocky crater they were passing. "Diamond Head, that's what they call it."

He grinned at Indy. "It's an old volcano. Did you know that a goddess used to live there? The locals told us stories about her— Pele, her name was." The veteran soldier shook his head. "I've known some hot babies in my time, but from the sound of it, she was too hot to handle." He chuckled. "Get her mad, and she'd burn you up!"

A launch left the docks. Indy could see puffs of smoke coming from the little vessel's steam engine.

"I guess that's a pilot coming to guide us in," he said.

As the launch came near, a deeply tanned man called up to some sailors who were letting down a rope ladder. "What ship is this?" he asked.

"*China Maid,* out of San Francisco," one of the crewmen replied.

"Oh, a humorist, huh?" the man on the launch yelled. "I piloted in the *China Maid* myself the other day."

The pilot and the sailors shot hot words back and forth. Finally, the captain and first mate were sent for.

"What's all this about?" the captain demanded. His eyes were bloodshot, and he looked even more whiskery than usual. Probably he'd gotten very little sleep after Indy's cries had wakened him the night before.

"Man doesn't believe we're the *China Maid*," one of the sailors reported.

"Bring him up here," the captain ordered. He stabbed a finger at his first mate. "You go get our papers."

The pilot was taken aback to find himself arguing with the ship's captain. "I thought the sailors were only joking," he said. "But I really did pilot the *China Maid* into its berth. So what vessel is this, really?"

At first, the captain stared as if the pilot had lost his mind. Then he lost his temper. "This *is* the *China Maid*!" he shouted. "I ought to know. After all, I've only been her master for the last six years."

Now the first mate appeared with an armload of papers.

The pilot looked through them, frowning. "The real *China Maid* had papers as well." He fingered the rather tattered log. "Better kept, too."

"Is this vessel you guided in still in port?" the captain demanded, red-faced.

The pilot glanced back at the docks and shrugged. "I guess they loaded their coal and sailed on."

The captain's ruddy face went purple. "You mean some vessel pretending to be us loaded our coal and sailed away? But that's *our* coal—prepaid and all!" He leaned forward until he was almost nose to nose with the pilot. "Son," he snarled, "you're going to guide us into one of the territorial berths. Then you're going to fetch the harbor authorities and someone from the Farron coal yards."

He rubbed his face vigorously, as if trying to make his whiskers—and a lot of other problems—go away.

"No coal," he muttered. "And we're completely out. It could take days for approval from the mainland to buy more. How am I supposed to go on to China?"

As soon as the boat docked, the captain headed off to talk with local officials.

That left the first mate in charge of disembarking the passengers. As Indy and his father reached the gangplank, Professor Jones turned to the mate. "Do you think this coal situation has something to do with the bomb last night?"

Indy rolled his eyes. He couldn't believe Dad would ask such an obvious question. Ever since he'd heard the pilot, Indy knew there had to be a connection. It looked as if their coal had been stolen. What better way to hide the theft than to blow up the real *China Maid*?

The only problem was that Indy had no idea who the thieves might be. Or why they would want to masquerade as this old boat.

"It could be. We don't know. But we've got the bomb locked in the captain's safe," the first mate said. "I suppose there'll be police, or someone, to investigate. In fact, they may want to question you. Do we know where you'll be?"

"It looks as if we'll be at the Moana." Professor Jones gave the name of one of the two hotels that had been recommended to the passengers.

A couple of seamen shouldered the Joneses' trunks, and they all headed down the gangplank.

"I hope we'll have no other surprises on this journey," the professor said.

"What more could—?" Indy began. Then his voice died away. A new surprise already awaited them down on the dock. Among the few bystanders were two people who should have been five thousand miles away in New York City.

Indy blinked in astonishment at none other than his Aunt Mary. And beside her was the beautiful blond girl who a year and a half ago had stolen Indy's heart—Lizzie Ravenall!

Chapter 3

"Henry!" Aunt Mary called up. She waved gaily from the dock. Professor Jones stumbled to a stop. A dumbstruck expression spread across his face.

Aunt Mary's thin features grew stern. She looked every inch the schoolteacher she used to be. "Honestly, Henry," she said, "what a surprise! When we heard that a Professor Henry Jones and a Henry Jones, Junior, had arrived on the latest ship, Lizzie suggested we go and see if it could be you."

She sniffed. "I assured her that was quite impossible, as you hadn't written that you were coming." She glared at the professor. "Surely you knew we were in Oahu. I wrote months ago to tell you that Lizzie and I were planning on sailing here."

"Ah," the professor said lamely. "You see, Mary, we haven't been back to Princeton in quite some time. And I'm afraid the mail sometimes lags behind our travels."

"Yes, I'm sure." Aunt Mary turned grim eyes in Indy's direction, which caused his spirits to drop like a rock. Although she was actually a second cousin once removed, Aunt Mary had acted more like a parent to Indy. She'd determinedly set to work "improving his mind," as she put it.

If the professor's pop quizzes were sometimes difficult, Aunt Mary's were torture. Professor Jones taught whatever caught his attention at the moment. Aunt Mary, however, questioned Indy on things she thought every fifteen-year-old should know.

Dad's interests had taught Indy a lot of odd things, from the history of the Norman kings of Sicily to Arabic. But he didn't know a great deal about some school subjects.

Lizzie Ravenall saw the look on Indy's face. "Why, Indy!" she called up. "I'd almost think you weren't glad to see me."

Keep calm, Indy told himself as he followed his father down the swaying gang-plank. Say something nice, and don't make a fool of yourself.

He'd met Lizzie Ravenall twice before, and each time, she'd almost gotten both of them killed. First she'd taken Indy along on a search through America's Eastern sea-board to recover her grandfather's fortune. Then, in New York City, they'd faced an ancient curse, fought a greedy millionaire—and met an eight-hundred-year-old ghost!

Both times, Lizzie had managed to talk Indy into doing things even *he* wouldn't nor-mally do. Indy couldn't quite explain why, not even to himself. But one look into those brilliant blue eyes set in that Greek-goddess face, and his brain shut off. Not to mention that his tongue suddenly felt a couple of sizes too large for his mouth.

Indy felt that way now as he reached the dock. "H-hi, Lizzie. What a surprise."

Great, he thought. You'll really impress her with *that*.

"A very *nice* surprise," he added.

Another girl stood on the dock. She was about the same age as Lizzie—nineteen—

and pretty enough. She had straw-colored hair and pink-and-white features, like a Dresden doll in a toy shop. But beside Lizzie, she looked washed out.

"Constanze Rademacher, may I present Professor Henry Jones and his son, Henry Junior." Lizzie grinned. "He prefers to be called Indy."

"Choosing to be nicknamed after our old family dog," Indy's father muttered.

"Excuse me?" Constanze said.

"Dad said there was a lot of fog," Indy said desperately. "We had a lot of fog on the voyage out."

Lizzie took pity on Indy and changed the subject. "Stanzi and I became such good friends at Barnard College," she said, "that she invited me for a summer visit here in Hawaii." Lizzie smiled. "And I asked Miss Jones to come along as chaperone."

"But classes must surely have begun again by now," Professor Jones said.

"They have," Lizzie admitted. "But with the start of the war, Stanzi decided to stay close to her parents. As for me..."

"I'm afraid Lizzie gave us a bit of a

scare," Aunt Mary said. "Shortly before we were supposed to leave, she came down with some sort of tropical fever. But I'm glad to say she's feeling much better now."

"My parents sent me to offer you an invitation," Stanzi said. "You are welcome to stay with us while you are here." A little frown came to her face. "Since there seems to be a problem with coal for your vessel, it might be a good idea."

"But you're already putting up Lizzie and Mary. We wouldn't want to inconvenience you—" Professor Jones began.

"I don't think Stanzi's family would mind." Lizzie glanced at her friend. "You haven't seen the Rademacher mansion yet. How much sugar does your family ship out of Hawaii, Stanzi?"

"Our company is one of the five biggest in the islands," Stanzi Rademacher said proudly. "Don't worry about space, Professor Jones. As Lizzie says, we have lots of it."

"Well," Indy's father said, "let me just inform the first mate."

While the professor went back up the

gangplank, Indy told the story of the strange bomb.

Stanzi's blue eyes opened wide. "How terrible!" she said. "It must have something to do with the war. Such awful things have been happening in the world."

Lizzie had a different interest. "You actually climbed up the mast? I'd have loved to do that."

Aunt Mary cleared her throat. "There are some things, Elizabeth, that young ladies simply do not do."

From the tone of Aunt Mary's voice—and the look on Lizzie's face—Indy could tell that those words had been heard a lot lately.

An open carriage awaited the party at the foot of the docks. As they rode through downtown Honolulu, Indy felt a little disappointed. He'd always thought of Hawaii as exotic, a land of grass huts and palm trees.

But the three-story buildings on either side of Fort Street were brick and wood, like the ones in any American town.

Oh, the businessmen were a bit different—Indy occasionally saw the square, dark features of a native Hawaiian, and a number of Asian faces. He'd heard that Honolulu had a thriving Chinatown. But even so, most people were dressed in drab American-style suits.

A streetcar came clanging by, and Indy spotted several of what his father called "those newfangled automobiles." He sighed. Honolulu looked just like home!

Then Stanzi made him feel a bit more as if he were in a land that had once been a foreign country. "We used to have a big house just *mauka* of here," she said.

"What?" said Indy.

Lizzie laughed. "In Hawaiian, *mauka* means 'toward the mountains.' *Makai* means 'toward the sea.'"

Indy repeated the words. "Mah-oo-kah. Mah-kie."

"Locally, that generally means north and south," Lizzie went on. "West is *Ewa*. That was the name of an old village to the west of town. East is *Waikiki*, where we're going. Just wait till you see!"

Chapter 4

The horses pulling the carriage set a brisk pace. Soon the group left the city behind. They rolled along a broad avenue shaded by palms and by other trees that Indy couldn't identify. The air grew thick with the smells of flowers and greenery.

A pink stone hotel building rose up before them, and beyond—

Indy sucked in a breath. For two miles, unreal blue water beat against a crescent of golden sand framed by green-clad hills. Farther in the distance loomed the scarred gray-and-black volcanic hulk of Diamond Head.

"Some view, isn't it?" Lizzie crowed. "A number of families have estates out here."

The carriage turned off the road and made its way through tall cast-iron gates. The party passed through lush tropical gardens until they finally reached a three-story mansion made from blocks of pinkish coral.

Indy saw what Lizzie had meant—the Rademachers had enough room to put up everyone on board the *China Maid*.

But there seemed to be plenty of visitors already, he noticed. A number of young men in uniform—navy-blue jackets and white trousers—stood on the wide open porches that circled each floor of the mansion.

The men all waved and called hello to Stanzi and Lizzie—in German, Indy noticed.

"Although I was born here, my family came from Germany," Stanzi said, smiling. "As you might guess from our name." Her smile faded as she looked at the men. "We shipped our sugar on German freighters—but now they're trapped here."

"Trapped?" Indy repeated.

"The war isn't being fought just in Europe," Lizzie said. "It's everywhere."

Stanzi nodded. "British and other Allied warships have begun seizing German vessels. Eight German ships made it to Honolulu. They've asked to be interned."

Lizzie turned to Indy to explain. "Since the U.S. is neutral, the German ships can apply to our government for protection. Of course, the ships and their crews will be stuck here until the war ends."

Lizzie proceeded to point out various officers and to identify which ships they came from.

"It doesn't look as if the men are having too tough a time." Indy's jealous gaze swept over the crowd of admirers.

Lizzie merely laughed. "Oh, they're a bunch of bored sailors looking for some fun." She tapped Indy on the arm. "Let's get you squared away. Then I'll take you for a walk around."

Indy's trunk was quickly placed in an empty bedroom. Soon he and Lizzie were strolling along Waikiki Beach. Indy squinted against the dazzling glare from the sand and looked out to sea.

"The surf seems much wilder out there than it does here at the beach," he said.

"There's a coral reef out there," Lizzie

explained. "In fact, most of the islands are ringed by reefs. There just happens to be an opening at Honolulu. In Hawaiian, the name means 'sheltered bay.'"

"You seem to have learned a lot of Hawaiian," said Indy.

Lizzie gave him a sunny smile. "My favorite word is *aloha*. Depending on the circumstances, it means 'hello' or 'good-bye.'" She hesitated a second. "Or 'love.'"

Indy turned from the water to give her a glance. Where had she learned *that*?

Silently, they wandered past another big estate with even more beautiful gardens. Lizzie steered them toward a smaller building. "This is the Outrigger Canoe Club," she said. "It's dedicated to the ancient Hawaiian sports of canoeing and surf-riding."

"Surf-riding?" Indy repeated doubtfully.

"Oh, it's great fun!" Lizzie said enthusiastically. "You ride on top of the waves on just a little board! I wish we had it back on the mainland—maybe someday." She headed to the clubhouse, where a dark and handsome young man stood polishing a ten-foot-tall piece of shaped lumber—one of those surf-riding boards, Indy figured.

"Lizzie!" the young man said with a dazzling smile. His black hair was slicked back from swimming, and his Polynesian features were rugged and very handsome.

Uh-oh, thought Indy. Now I see where she's been learning so much Hawaiian.

"Indy Jones, meet Mike Halani," Lizzie said. "He's been teaching me to surf."

"*Aloha,*" Mike greeted them.

"Indy has just arrived," Lizzie said. "I think he's still getting used to Waikiki."

"I can see why a goddess would like to live here," Indy said, recalling the story Sergeant Warrick had told him on the ship. He nodded toward the bulk of Diamond Head.

"So, you know of Pele's visit here?" Mike said with a smile. "She tried each of the islands. But each time she created a crater with her magic digging stick, the sea put out her fires—until she finally came to the big island of Hawaii. That's where my family comes from."

"What brings you to Oahu?" Indy asked.

Mike shrugged. "There are better jobs— and the surfing is good. At one time, only royalty could surf the Waikiki coast."

Lizzie stepped to the clubhouse door. "Is it all right if I—"

Mike shrugged. "Sure."

Indy gave Lizzie a puzzled look as she went inside. Mike peered off across the water. "Oh, good one!" he cried. "Look at him coming in!"

Indy followed Mike's gaze. A human figure seemed to be standing on the crest of a wave. But Indy quickly realized that the figure was actually standing on one of those ten-foot boards. The rider put his arms out straight in front of him and went into a crouch as his board suddenly cut to the right. He seemed to fly across the water, barely skimming the surface.

"That's surf-riding?" Indy said. "I never—" But words failed him as Lizzie came back out. Indy gasped. "Where did you get that— that bathing costume?" he asked, choking.

Indy liked to think of himself as modern. After all, this *was* 1914. But Lizzie was definitely dressed on the skimpy side. This costume left most of her arms bare, there was hardly any skirt, and the pantaloons ended well above her ankles. "You—you're not even wearing stockings," he said, gulping.

"Oh, don't be such a fuddy-duddy," Lizzie said. "I was hoping to get one of those new one-piece swimming suits."

Indy had seen pictures of the scandalous new suits. Then his father had confiscated that particular newspaper. The thought of Lizzie in such formfitting attire made him dizzy.

"Come on. We're going surf-riding. Mike and I will show you how it's done." Lizzie glanced at her Hawaiian friend. "Do you have anything Indy could go swimming in?"

Mike wore a typical man's swimming jersey. He looked Indy over. "Sure, I think I have something that will fit."

The top and bottom of Indy's suit didn't exactly match, but Lizzie seemed to think he looked fine. "I declare, you just keep growing up and up," she remarked.

His face flaming, Indy turned to examine the surfing board. It had been carved into a shape somewhere between a fish and a gravestone. And when Indy hefted it, he found it surprisingly heavy.

"Fräulein Ravenall." A voice interrupted Indy's investigation. He turned to see yet another young German sailing officer. The man was handsome enough, with short-cropped blond hair. But his stocky build and thick neck gave him a bull-like appearance. Now his head was down, and he was scowling at Lizzie and Mike.

"It is not proper," he said in heavily accented English, "to be with a *native*." The officer made it sound like a dirty word.

"Mike is my friend," Lizzie said angrily. "And he has agreed to teach me and my friend Indy how to surf."

She glanced at Indy. "Leutnant Kurt Messer, this is Henry Jones, just off the *China Maid*."

Kurt Messer gave Indy a stiff nod and marched off down the beach, muttering in German. "Just as well I'll be leaving on the *Ostwind*," Indy heard the man say.

That's odd, Indy thought. When Lizzie pointed out the officers at the Rademacher mansion, she mentioned what ships they were from. He frowned. There had been no mention of a ship called the *Ostwind*.

Chapter 5

Indy returned to the Rademacher mansion with salt in his hair and a grin on his face. Mike Halani had told Indy he'd done well for a *malahini*—a newcomer to the sport. His lessons in surf-riding had been fun. The sensation of actually traveling on a wave had been—well, thrilling. And Indy had been impressed at how well Lizzie had mastered her board.

Only when he was washing up for dinner did Indy realize that Aunt Mary would have a fit if she found out what Lizzie was up to. That girl had done it again.

During dinner, Indy discovered that Lizzie had more amusements planned. She skillfully led the conversation to the ancient volcanoes in the area—Diamond Head, and the Punchbowl crater *mauka* of Honolulu.

"All of the Hawaiian Islands are of volcanic origin," Aunt Mary said. "I believe there are several active volcanoes on the large island of Hawaii."

"That is true," Stanzi said. "In fact, Lizzie and I were going to suggest a visit to the volcanoes." She turned to Professor Jones. "I understand the problems of coaling the *China Maid* will delay you for some days. This would be an opportunity to see a most interesting natural display."

Stanzi's father, a plump, pink old gentleman with a white walrus mustache, nodded. "*Ja.* There is even a good hotel set on the lip of one of the volcanoes. You ought to go."

"I should like to accompany the party," announced Kurt Messer, who was dining with the family. "That is, if such a journey is permitted for those of us who are interned."

Herr Rademacher chuckled. "I do not think you will sail off on the little inter-island steamer," he said. "There should be no problem."

Lizzie smiled radiantly. "I think I know where I can find a local guide."

The next afternoon, seven people boarded the small steamboat for Hilo, Hawaii. Besides Indy, Professor Jones, and Aunt Mary, Lizzie and Stanzi, Kurt Messer, and Mike Halani climbed the gangplank.

The German lieutenant gave Mike several dirty looks. Then he found a new annoyance—the eighth passenger on the boat.

"Sidney Pilkington," the newcomer introduced himself in a cultured British accent. "Joining your party, if no one objects. Doctor of ornithology, don't you know."

"You study birds?" Aunt Mary asked.

"That's it!" said Pilkington. "Spot on!" The ornithologist had a round face, half tanned, half sunburned. He removed a pith helmet better suited for exploring jungles than for a boat trip, and fanned himself. His white hair was mostly gone on top, and he had a big, white, droopy mustache.

To Indy, the man almost looked funny. Pilkington was the sort of Englishman who appeared in American comedy plays. He'd be bumbling, and called something like "the Major."

Kurt Messer, however, did not find Pilkington funny. He kept giving the Englishman suspicious looks. But then, their countries were at war.

The two-day journey to Hilo passed uneventfully. But Indy noticed one odd thing. Messer and Pilkington were quietly keeping an eye on each other. If Messer stood on the upper deck, Pilkington was at the bottom of the companionway, watching. If Pilkington stayed in the dining room talking to the ladies, Messer stood in the doorway, studying the scene.

But the only real unpleasantness happened right before they left the ship. Pilkington had brought his gear onto the deck for unloading. Atop his trunk were a set of expensive long-range binoculars and a camera case.

"What are these?" Messer demanded. He pointed at them rudely.

"Why, that's my equipment, old boy," Pilkington replied. He sounded a little annoyed.

"Best way to watch birds, don't you see. And sometimes I can snap a picture of them."

"Oh, yes," Messer replied, his voice angry. "The English love to watch the birds. I remember stories of a Sidney Reilly who watched the birds all around Port Arthur. That was ten years ago, right before the Russo-Japanese War."

Indy's ears perked up. He'd read that British spies had helped the Japanese prepare for war. Supposedly, an agent had checked out and photographed the harbor defenses. That had cleared the way for a Japanese sneak attack that crippled the Russian Far East Fleet.

He looked at Sidney Pilkington with new eyes. Could the silly Englishman merely be putting on an act? He was an older man, but not too old to be serving as a British officer. Why was he hanging around in Hawaii with a war on, anyway?

Pilkington began fanning himself with his pith helmet. His pinkish face had a perplexed expression. "Don't know what you're talking about, old bean. Was this Reilly chap some sort of amateur ornithologist? Never seen his name in the professional journals."

When the steamboat chugged into Hilo harbor an hour later, Indy realized that this was a much smaller town than Honolulu. Three-story American-style buildings were clustered by the dock; they seemed hemmed in by the green mountains rising as a backdrop. But in the distance, Indy thought he could make out some native grass shacks.

He also noticed several American warships riding at anchor.

When he asked about them, Stanzi answered, "Oh, Hilo is the main naval base hereabouts."

Kurt Messer gave him a superior smile. "I understand your navy has been trying to build a new base near Honolulu—what is the place?"

"Pearl Harbor." Stanzi supplied the name.

Messer went on. "They dredged an entrance for ships, but when they tried to build a dry dock for repairing vessels, it collapsed. Apparently they were building on coral. It just wasn't strong enough."

"All the work had to stop," Stanzi said. "And they've been keeping all sorts of supplies in Papa's warehouses."

Indy glanced at his father's glazed expression and sighed. Professor Jones's interest in naval affairs ended with the Battle of Lepanto in 1571.

"Mike mentioned the Pearl Harbor disaster," Lizzie said. "But he has a different theory." She smiled and nodded to him.

Mike Halani shrugged. "They were building on the home of the shark god," he said.

"Really!" Aunt Mary said with a sniff. "You can't seriously be talking about pagan gods that way. I was given to understand that Christian missionaries had converted the Hawaiians."

"Oh, I'm a Christian," Mike assured her. "But I also know our Hawaiian gods. Only a *haole* would have built there."

"How-lay?" Aunt Mary repeated with a puzzled look on her face.

"That's Hawaiian for 'foreigner,'" Lizzie said. "Specifically, for foreigners like us."

Raising her eyes to heaven, Aunt Mary let the matter drop.

Hours later, the group of eight mounted rented horses for the trip to the volcano. Fog shrouded the valleys, hiding Hilo and all traces of civilization. As they climbed above the fog, Indy looked up to find enormous roiling clouds sailing above them. The vista made him feel like a very small bug in this land of the gods.

Messer obviously didn't feel the same way. He trotted his horse up front to join Mike Halani, and immediately started an argument.

"I don't know why Kurt seems so annoyed at Mike being our guide," Stanzi said. "After all, Mike's family comes from this area." She rode ahead to try and calm things down.

Indy glanced back to the end of the procession, where Pilkington and Professor Jones were riding. Then he turned to Lizzie.

"You missed quite a show on deck this morning," he told her. "Kurt Messer didn't like the look of Pilkington's high-power binoculars and camera. He all but accused him of being a British spy."

"I wouldn't be surprised." The voice came from behind them.

Indy twisted in his saddle to see that Aunt Mary had ridden closer. She was perched sidesaddle on an elderly horse, but her thin face was confident as she shook her head.

"I'm a bit of a bird-watcher back home," she said. "In the spring and fall, I like to get up in the Adirondacks and follow the migrations. But when I try to chat with this so-called ornithologist, he either changes the subject or gets his facts wrong."

And Aunt Mary, Indy knew all too well, had no patience with people who got their facts wrong.

"I don't know *what* that man is," she said, "but he doesn't know beans about birds."

Chapter 6

"A spy?" Lizzie's blue eyes lit up.

Indy had the sinking feeling he should have said nothing. Who knew what Lizzie's sense of adventure might lead to? "We'd better not mention this to anyone," he said.

"Especially to Kurt Messer." Lizzie gave him a grin.

"As a mere suspicion, it might cause trouble," Aunt Mary said in agreement.

Indy continued to worry as the group rode thirty miles—from valleys crammed with jungle ferns, to gentle but rocky slopes. "Where's the volcano?" he asked.

"You're climbing it," Mike called back. "This is Kilauea." He made it sound like kee-loo-*way*-ah.

Lizzie smiled. "From what Mike tells me, Hawaiian volcanoes tend to be flat and wide. Lava spills from vents in the side."

Above them, the grass and low scrub disappeared in a huge splotch of gray. It looked as if some giant had poured paint on the mountainside. But Indy knew it was stone—lava that had flowed, then dried.

Mike reached a rocky ridge and reined in his horse. As the others came up, they saw why he'd stopped. They were standing on the lip of the volcano's crater.

Indy could usually estimate distances. But atop this sheer drop, he had no clue to the height of the clifflike walls rising on the far side of the flat gray-green stone floor below.

Lizzie pointed. "I wonder what could be in that box over there on the crater rim."

"Box?" Indy peered. "That's no box. That's a shack!"

Suddenly, the view snapped into a new, much larger scale. "That wall must be a good two miles away," Indy said in shock. "And the floor must be four hundred feet down."

Mike nodded. "That's the volcano observatory over there—it went up in 1912. Kilauea is about two and a half miles long and two miles wide." He pointed off through some steamy-looking clouds. "Over that way is Halemaumau, where Pele now lives." He made it sound like ha-lay-*mau*-mau.

In the distance, Indy got a vague glimpse of what seemed to be a lake. But from what he could see through the boiling mist, it was orange and not blue.

"Let's move on," said Mike. "I don't know about all of you, but I'm getting hungry." He led them away from the lookout point and along a path that ran through straggling brush. Then, in the middle of nowhere, they found themselves facing a row of hedges and a long, white-painted wooden building.

An elderly man with a bristly gray mustache stood on the front porch. "Welcome to Volcano House!" he called. "I'm the owner—call me Uncle George. You must be the Rademacher party."

Indy and the others signed in. "Check the register later," Mike told him. "Mark Twain stayed here back in the 1860s."

"From *Huckleberry Finn* and *Tom Sawyer*

to volcanoes," Indy said, laughing.

The lobby of the hotel was very welcoming, with a big, roaring blaze in the fireplace. "They've kept a fire burning there for nearly fifty years," Mike said. "It's not just tradition, either. Nights get cold up here on top of the mountain. You'll see when we go down into the volcano tonight!"

"Tonight? Why not wait until tomorrow?" Professor Jones asked.

Mike grinned. "Better show at night."

Uncle George brushed a thoughtful finger over his mustache as Pilkington signed in. "We have only a dozen rooms here in the main building," he said. "Would you consider sharing a room?" He turned to Messer. "Perhaps this gentleman—"

"No!" the Englishman and German said together.

"First time they've agreed on anything," Lizzie whispered.

They finally settled in, with Pilkington and Messer at opposite ends of the hall. As Indy and his dad left their room for dinner, they saw Messer standing in his doorway, glaring toward Pilkington's room.

But the Britisher walked out of his room and down the hall without seeming to notice.

He's either the coolest character I've ever seen, Indy thought, or a real boob.

After dinner, the visitors slipped on jackets and gathered at the front porch. Mike Halani stood waiting with a lantern and a walking stick.

"It's a three-mile walk," he announced. "The trail is well marked, and easy enough— as long as we stay together."

The sun had gone down behind neighboring mountains by the time the group set off. Sharp shadows had already formed in Kilauea crater. But the glow of Mike's lantern, along with some faint moonlight, led the tourists on.

Lizzie lagged behind, picking berries off a stand of bushes. She'd filled her hat with a most luscious-looking fruit. "I'll bet these are good to eat," she told Indy.

Mike suddenly appeared. "You haven't eaten any of these *ohelo* berries, have you?" He put the accent on the second syllable: oh-*hay*-low. He frowned. "They only grow on the sides of volcanoes, and they're sacred to Pele. You're supposed to toss half of what you pick into Halemaumau as a sacrifice."

"I thought they'd make a nice treat," Lizzie said. "We haven't eaten any."

"*Haole*s," Mike muttered, moving on.

"Why did he make it sound like *I* was going to eat some?" Indy asked.

"Food," said an unfamiliar voice. Indy and Lizzie both jumped. The voice appeared to have come from the shadows off the trail.

Indy spun around and saw an old woman. She seemed to step from a crack between two rocks. Though her hair was gray and her face wrinkled, she stood tall and proud in a sarong-like garment. Her gaze seemed to burn as she looked at them.

"I am hungry," the woman said simply.

"We have no food," Indy apologized.

"Except for these." Lizzie held out her hat full of *ohelo* berries. "Our guide said we should sacrifice half to Pele." She bit her lip. She was not happy about annoying Mike. "But if you're hungry—"

"Hungry," the old woman said. She took the berries, hat and all, then vanished.

"Where'd she go?" Indy stepped up to the crack. It disappeared in shadows. And it seemed to go deep into the ground.

"Where did she *come from*?" Lizzie corrected. "Nobody lives in a volcano." She gulped, and looked Indy straight in the eye. "Except Pele." Lizzie grabbed Indy's arm, and rushed them back to the group.

Indy began to chuckle. But then he remembered his last adventure with Lizzie: They had met a ghost.

The group reached the gray lava floor of the crater. In some places, the rock had an almost rippling surface, as if a moving puddle had abruptly frozen. At another point, Mike detoured around more cindery rock, where sharp, jagged edges stuck up.

"The rippling rock is called *pahoehoe*," Mike said. To Indy, it sounded like *pah*-ho-way-ho-way.

"The sharp rock is *aa*," Mike went on. The word sounded like *ah*-ah.

"Why is it called that?" Professor Jones asked.

"What noise would you make if *you* stepped on it?" Mike said with a grin.

As the sky darkened, Indy noticed an orange glow ahead of them.

"Uncle George told me that Halemaumau is running a little high right now," Mike said. "This should be interesting."

It turned out that the glow came from a hole in the ground—the "lake" Indy had seen from the summit. It *was* a lake—maybe half a mile in diameter—a lake of boiling lava.

As the party stared, some of the liquid stone turned solid. It looked like the scum of ice that forms on a puddle in wintertime. A second later, the stone sank back into the bubbling lava and melted again.

Lizzie's eyes were wide with awe, her face ruddy in the glow of the molten rock.

"If you want to get on Pele's good side," Mike said, "throw those berries now."

"I can't," Lizzie said. Her face turned even redder from embarrassment. "I gave them away."

Lizzie told the story of the strange woman. Aunt Mary began grumping about people who gave away perfectly good hats.

Mike, however, seemed impressed. "It's

said that sometimes, before an eruption, Pele appears as an old woman."

Lizzie glanced at Indy. Professor Jones shrugged. "An interesting myth," he said.

"I'm more interested in history," Aunt Mary said. "This fire pit—isn't it mentioned in the missionary story? When the Hawaiian princess defied the false goddess? A priestess of Pele came waving a bark parchment. But the princess put her faith in the Bible. She took some of those berries and ate them all, depending on her faith in Jehovah to protect her."

"Is that true?" Lizzie said.

"Well, some of it is," Mike said. "In 1823, Princess Kapiolani visited Kilauea and went down into the crater. Lava was flowing, and several people warned her that Pele might eat her. Kapiolani said that if Pele ate her, folks could continue to worship the goddess. But Kapiolani was a Christian, and if Pele didn't eat her, she said, they should become Christians, too. She came through alive, and the local people converted to Christianity." He glanced at Aunt Mary. "I'm sorry, ma'am," he said. "There was nothing about priestesses or *ohelo* berries."

"I merely repeated what I read," Aunt Mary said. "What history are you quoting?"

"Family history," Mike replied. "My great-grandfather was one of the people who warned the princess." He smiled. "And, although we became Christians, my family still counts Pele as an ancestor."

"Superstition," Aunt Mary muttered with a sniff.

But her sniff suddenly turned into a choke. As if to punish her, a bubble of deadly gas began rising from the lava.

"Once Pele got angry and suffocated a whole army of warriors," Mike said when he had stopped coughing from the gas. "They were marching past Kilauea when the volcano erupted. You can still see the warriors' footprints in the ashes."

"Save the stories for fresher air," Lizzie said. "Too bad it's too dark to take some pictures with your camera, Dr. Pilkington."

She looked around. "Doctor? Doctor? Where *is* Dr. Pilkington?"

Indy frowned as he peered into the darkness. "And where's Kurt Messer?"

Chapter 7

Mike grew concerned. "Pilkington was asking me about the Ring of Craters. It's a rough trail down the southern flank of the volcano. It leads toward the sea."

Worry filled his voice. "And to get to it, Pilkington would need to take another path that follows ledges up to the crater rim. But it's dangerous up on top at night! With the fissures in the ground, he could get badly hurt!"

Especially if Kurt Messer has anything to say about it, Indy thought grimly. "We'd better find those two before they go too high," he said out loud.

Mike handed his lantern to Professor Jones. "We've seen the best of the display.

Could you get the ladies back to the hotel? Indy and I will start a search."

"I believe I can find the way," the professor said.

"And if he can't, I will," Aunt Mary assured them. "I've got a very good sense of direction."

The darkness got ever deeper as Mike and Indy moved away from Halemaumau. Indy reached into his pocket and brought out an electric torch. "I was saving this for the journey back," he said. "But it looks as if we can use it now."

With the flashlight to show the way, the pair of rescuers made quick progress to the trail along the ledge.

They tramped on until they reached the clifflike crater wall. Mike was disappointed— and beginning to look worried. "I was hoping we'd catch up with them by now. From here on, the path is even steeper."

It *was* a steep climb, Indy discovered. Maybe Messer could take this route, he thought. But a man of Pilkington's age would have to be crazy to play mountaineer—especially at night. Indy was breathing hard when he heard a scrabbling among the rocks below them.

"Who's there?" he called.

"Who did you expect?" Lizzie's voice replied. "Did you really think I was going to go back to the hotel with the old folks?"

Indy glanced at his guide. "It would have been so much easier," he muttered.

"She may as well come along," Mike said with a sigh. "We can't leave her alone."

The next stretch of path was a little easier. "I hope they're okay," said Lizzie. "Maybe they got lost...or worse. It's so dark and desolate up here. This isn't a well-traveled route, that's for sure."

"There are better trails, but they're the long way around," Mike said. "This way is more direct."

It's also a nice, isolated place to question a British spy, Indy thought. Or, for that matter, for a British spy to question a suspicious German officer.

"There are some sights up here," Mike said. "Lesser craters and funnels dot this side of Kilauea. Maybe that's what they came to see. But they're nothing compared with the main crater." He paused. "Oddly enough, Pilkington seemed most interested in the view of the sea."

"He wants to look at the sea by night?" Indy said. "He could have done that last night on the boat."

"I guess he wanted to see the ocean from this shore," Mike said. "I don't know why anyone would want to come here. We call this part of the coast the Kau desert."

The track grew worse again, and they stopped talking to scramble up a rock wall. "Idiots," Indy muttered.

"Pilkington or Messer?" Lizzie asked a little breathlessly.

"Us," Indy wheezed. "For looking for them."

They reached a thin rocky ledge. Mike stood leaning on his walking stick. "Let's rest," he said.

"Could you tell us some more about Pele?" Lizzie asked as they sat down. "You said she appears as an old woman. What does she look like?"

Indy glanced at Lizzie. She seemed very interested in Pele after their strange encounter on the way to Halemaumau. Maybe it was just the spirit of the place. The inside of the crater did seem like another world.

"Oh, my distinguished ancestor has many faces," Mike said. "Sometimes she's an old hag; sometimes she's a beautiful young woman. Pele was young and beautiful when she challenged a pair of chiefs to a sporting contest. They realized who she was and made a dash for the sea. She sent lava after them—and they couldn't outrun it."

"That's cheerful." Indy stood up and began flashing his light around. "Too bad this is all rock. I'd feel better if we could find a footprint...."

He stood at the brink of the ledge, and his voice trailed off as the flashlight illuminated a narrower ledge below them. The edge of the beam caught the sole of a hiking shoe. Indy aimed the beam at the shoe and up along a dusty leg to reveal a still form lying on the ledge. He gasped when he realized who he was staring at—Dr. Sidney Pilkington.

"Hey, Pilkington!" he yelled.

There was no answer. The Britisher

remained as he was. He lay on his side, his face away from the rescue party on the ledge above.

"Out of my way!" Lizzie cried. "I've had first-aid training." Before Indy could stop her, she'd gone over the edge, skittering down the slope toward Pilkington.

"Watch out!" Indy called. All he could do was aim his flashlight to light her path. Lizzie reached the lower shelf of rock and anxiously edged over to reach Pilkington. She dropped to one knee and placed her fingers on his wrist.

When she looked up, there was relief all over her face. "There's a pulse. He's alive!" she called. Then she looked concerned again. "He's talking, but he's not making much sense."

Pilkington moaned, and Lizzie bit her lip. Her gaze settled on his left leg. "I'm not sure, but it looks as if his leg may be broken. I'd say he took a pretty bad fall."

"We've got to get him to a doctor," said Indy. "But he may need a splint."

"Here—this should work," said Mike. He passed his wooden walking stick to Indy, who broke it in two. Then he tossed the pieces to Lizzie—carefully. They wouldn't do much good if he overshot the narrow ledge. Lizzie gently bound up the leg with strips of cloth torn from her petticoats.

"I wonder what happened," said Lizzie. "And where is his bird-watching equipment—the expensive binoculars and the camera?"

"Good question," said Indy. He shivered, thinking for a moment of the odd woman they'd met earlier that evening. "Who knows—a sacrifice to Pele, maybe?"

Even as Indy spoke, something clattered down from above him. It was the very set of binoculars Lizzie had just mentioned. And a second later, the camera came whizzing by.

Looks like Pele doesn't like us, Indy thought. What *does* she want—a human sacrifice?

Then he heard a slithering, rumbling rush overhead. Indy gulped. Maybe a human sacrifice was *exactly* what Pele wanted. The falling camera and binoculars were nothing compared with the rock slide that was now in the works!

Chapter 8

Indy threw himself over the lip of the ledge and plunged down to the rocky shelf below. He beat the worst of the falling rock and braced himself as a shield over Lizzie. Luckily, most of the slide flew out and past them. But several rocks hit Indy, with one large enough to draw a cry of pain.

Seeing that Indy was shielding Lizzie and that there was little room on the lower ledge, Mike took cover.

Lizzie looked up at Indy with wide eyes. "I thought you had fallen," she said in an unsteady voice.

Indy forgot about being hurt, and smiled at Lizzie. But his happiness ended as she went on. "How could you do something so stupid? You didn't have to jump! We'd have been fine down here."

The spatter of rocks stopped, and Indy rubbed his bruised shoulder. "I was afraid a bigger rock might be on its way down."

As if to underline his words, they heard a low, grinding noise, like a boulder about to give way upslope. Or, Indy suddenly thought, like someone trying to *push* a boulder loose.

"We've got to get out of here!" he exclaimed with a gasp.

Indy looked down at Pilkington. There was no way the Britisher could move on his own. Gritting his teeth, Indy lifted one of Pilkington's arms, draped it over his shoulder, and stood. The man's restless muttering turned to groans as Indy managed to get him upright. Lizzie grabbed Pilkington's other arm, and they began moving along the narrow ledge.

The Englishman's sorry condition slowed them to an awkward shuffle. And with every step, the grinding of rock against rock grew louder. At the rate they were moving, Indy could feel his way. So he snapped off his flashlight. Now he had both hands free for steadying Pilkington.

Also, Indy came to realize, they were less of a target without the flashlight. It suddenly became clear to Indy that Pilkington hadn't fallen from above. He had been pushed. And whoever had pushed him had tried to hide the evidence by starting a rock slide. But now an even bigger rock slide was needed to finish the job. Indy tried to move faster.

The groan of the rocks above suddenly turned to a shuddering roar. A huge boulder crashed against the upper ledge—just missing Mike Halani, who had scooted away as quickly as possible along the ledge. The boulder tumbled to the very rock shelf on which Indy, Lizzie, and Pilkington stood— and it landed on the spot they'd occupied just seconds ago.

Instantly, that section of ledge shattered. It was torn away by a welter of rocks traveling at express-train speed.

The next moment, Indy heard a cracking noise. The rock under his feet quivered, and the whole ledge started to give way!

Indy looked up, desperately seeking a handhold, and spotted something moving rapidly in the moonlight. It was a pair of hands reaching down to him. "Gotta get you up here," Mike Halani said. "And quick!"

Pilkington shrieked in pain as Indy and Lizzie heaved him up to Mike's outstretched arms. Then Indy helped Lizzie onto the sturdier rock shelf above. Indy scrambled to safety just as his perch crumbled away.

"I wanted to get off that ledge," said Indy, panting. "But not *that* fast!"

Mike managed to scout out a gentler route to get Pilkington down to the crater floor. But even on flatter ground, the Britisher wasn't easy to handle, for the lava here had frozen into flows that looked like coiled rope. That made for dozens of furrows and gullies that could easily be tripped on.

Bobbing lights appeared in the distance. Slowly, Indy made out the figures of several hotel workers carrying lanterns.

It turned out that as soon as Professor Jones had returned with the news of lost tourists, Uncle George had sent out a search party. Thankfully, Indy let the people from

Volcano House carry Pilkington to the hotel.

As Indy stood rubbing weary arms, he saw another figure come out of the darkness. Although this one didn't have a lantern, his stocky frame and jutting jaw gave his identity away.

"Leutnant Messer," Indy said. "Where were *you*?"

The German stood stock-still. "I became lost," he said after a moment's pause. "Luckily, I saw the lights here."

"Luckier than you know," Indy told him. "Dr. Pilkington wandered away and got hurt climbing the crater."

"*Ach!* But he is...alive?" Messer asked, his accent getting thicker.

"Yes. I'd say he beat the odds." Indy glared suspiciously at the German. "Miss Ravenall and I nearly got crushed by a rock slide while rescuing him. Did you hear or see any of that?"

"*Nein,*" Messer replied quickly, not meeting Indy's eyes. "Those cliffs seemed too dangerous."

"Gee, if that's how you felt, then I'm surprised you went off by yourself," Indy said.

"Come to think of it, why did you leave?"

Messer stiffened. "The world is supposed to be a certain way. Stone is stone, water is water. Rock is not supposed to flow like water. It is…unnatural!"

Indy had to agree with part of what Messer was saying. He'd gotten a queasy feeling as he stared into Halemaumau. The expression "rock-solid" would never be quite the same for him. But he couldn't call what he'd seen unnatural. It was just a part of nature that very few people got to see.

Messer stepped past him. "I bid you good night, Herr Jones. Fräulein."

Indy turned, and saw that Lizzie was standing nearby. Her hiking outfit was torn and dusty. She didn't even nod in response as Messer went by.

"I thought you'd be back up at the hotel by now," Indy said.

Lizzie shook her head. Her eyes gleamed. "No. I was waiting, just like you, for Messer to turn up."

"I wasn't waiting for the guy," Indy protested. "He just turned up."

"And you had some very interesting

questions for him," Lizzie purred. She was quite excited. "He must believe Pilkington is a spy, too! He all but confessed to what happened out there!"

"I didn't hear any confession," Indy said.

"But he couldn't look at you when you talked about the rock slide." Lizzie leaned forward. "That's just about the same as a confession."

"Tell that to the police and see how far you get." Indy was too tired to argue. He yawned as they set off for the hotel. "I guess we'll get the whole story when Pilkington wakes up."

"Yes," Lizzie said. She had a grim, determined look on her face. "Stanzi, your aunt, and I will sit up with him all night." She glanced at Indy. "To make *sure* he wakes up."

The next morning dawned foggy and chilly. As he stepped out of the hotel dining room and into the sun parlor, Indy was thankful for the warm breakfast he'd just eaten. Kurt Messer sat in a wood-and-wicker chair in front of the fire, reading the Hilo newspaper. "The *Emden* has struck again!" he said happily.

"Pardon?" Indy said.

"Ah, yes, you are behind on the local war news." Messer tapped the headline. "My country's Far East Squadron has sailed home to Germany to reinforce the main fleet. But Admiral Scheer left a raider behind—the cruiser *Emden*. She has been making much trouble for the Allies. Two days ago, she sank several freighters in the Indian Ocean."

Indy left Messer to his minor triumph and headed back upstairs. His father had assigned some reading for the day, and Indy wanted to get it over with.

Before he reached his room, however, a door popped open. Lizzie's face appeared, and she beckoned frantically. "He's awake!" she whispered hoarsely.

Rolling his eyes, Indy walked into Sidney Pilkington's room. One of the overstuffed chairs had been moved over beside the bed, to make a place for the volunteer nurses to rest. The patient was sitting up in bed. His normally pink face looked pale and bruised, and his splinted leg stuck out from the covers.

"I'm glad to see you, Mr. Jones," he said. "Miss Ravenall has been telling me some interesting things about you."

Now Indy realized there was another change in Sidney Pilkington. His bumbling-Englishman act was gone. It was as if his fall had knocked some sense into him.

Or, Indy thought, the mask has been dropped.

Pilkington seemed to read his mind. "That's right. I'm not a silly ornithologist. I'm an agent of His Majesty's government."

See? Lizzie's glance seemed to say. A spy!

"We'd had rumors of some sort of activity among the interned German sailors in Honolulu," Pilkington said. "When this Messer fellow left the city, I was assigned to follow him."

The British agent frowned. "I thought he might be trying to pass secret information about Allied shipping to a German commerce raider. You've heard of the *Emden*?"

Indy nodded.

"The coast to the south and west of

Mount Kilauea is barren. It would be very easy for a ship to come by night and receive a message. So I went to scan the area."

"That's why you sneaked away from our party," Indy said.

"Yes, while you were all staring at that fire pit. Looked like h—" He glanced at Lizzie. "Sorry—ladies present. Looked like Hades to me. But it offered an excellent chance for me to absent myself. And I figured I was already halfway there."

"Except you never made it all the way," Indy put in.

"Something—or someone—fell on me as I was climbing that ruddy crater. And now I'm laid up." Pilkington gestured toward his splinted leg. "I need your help, Mr. Jones. The British government needs your help."

He gave Indy a man-to-man look. "I know Messer is up to something, but I can't go to the authorities about it."

"Right," said Indy. "America is neutral, and your activities would be as illegal as Messer's."

"But a private citizen could help me. I thought of approaching your father, but frankly, he's a bit too bookish. Judging by what I've heard from Miss Ravenall, you're just the man I need."

"No," Indy said firmly.

Pilkington stared in shock. "How could you turn me down? How could you turn *England* down? You, who were educated there."

"I spent two terms in a British boarding school," Indy said. "When the boys weren't making fun of me for being a Yank, they were playing cruel practical jokes on a friend of mine. I have no reason to like England."

"You can't say you prefer the Germans!" Pilkington protested.

Indy shook his head. "I've had some run-ins with German spies." He wrinkled his nose in disgust. "Just like you Brits, they think the world belongs to them. Well, you can fight it out between yourselves. America is neutral, and Hawaii is part of America. I'm not going to help fight your little war here."

"Well, then, I will!" Lizzie said defiantly.

"Hah! Lizzie Ravenall, master spy." Indy

stomped out of the room and went to pick up his book.

By afternoon, the book lay shut in his lap. He'd read the same page three times, and it still didn't make any sense. Sighing, Indy went in search of Lizzie, book in hand.

He caught up with her in the garden. She looked terrifically excited—she was even trembling. "So, you didn't think I'd know what to do." Lizzie reached into her skirt pocket and took out a piece of paper.

"A telegram came for Kurt Messer from Hilo. And I copied it out. It has to be a secret message!"

Indy looked at Lizzie's scribbled words. "'The east wind blows tonight,'" he read. "Probably some kind of code." Then he stopped as a memory hit him.

"What? What is it?" Lizzie's eyes were eating up his face.

"Back in Honolulu, Messer mentioned leaving on a ship called the *Ostwind*. But there was no such ship in Honolulu harbor."

"So?" Lizzie said.

"*Ostwind* is German for 'east wind.'"

Chapter 9

"So the east wind in the message is a ship." Lizzie's eyes shone. "That decodes part of it. But where does the wind blow?"

Indy's stomach flip-flopped. "Lizzie, you won't do anything stu—"

"Oh, don't trouble your head about it, Mr. I'm-Not-Going-to-Fight-Any-Wars."

As Lizzie flounced off, Indy sighed. "I've got to learn to keep my big mouth shut," he muttered. "Especially when it comes to decoding secret messages."

"Ah, Junior," cried Professor Jones as he strolled down the garden path. "Glad to see you've got your reading there."

Indy tried again to focus on his book of Chinese history. It might as well have been *written* in Chinese for all the good it did him. He failed miserably on Dad's daily quiz.

Then Aunt Mary came to test Indy on a variety of high school topics. "Your father claims he's been tutoring you," she said in disgust. "But he has no *plan*. Some subjects are totally lacking. In others, you're doing college-level work."

"Really?" Indy said in surprise.

"Don't let it go to your head, young man," Aunt Mary promptly flattened him. "You'll never get into college unless you improve in the other subject areas. How about mathematics? Do you know algebra?"

Indy blinked. "Bone-setting? What has that got to do with math?"

"Eh?" Aunt Mary said in confusion.

"*Al jabr* is Arabic for the science of setting bones—or reuniting things."

"Really?" Aunt Mary thought for a second. "The name 'algebra' does come from the Arabic, I'm told. And that 'reuniting' idea could relate to making equations equal one another. Quite interesting, Henry."

Then she glared. "But if the name 'algebra' is so foreign to you, I suspect the subject matter is equally unknown."

Indy sighed. It's not enough to have problems with Lizzie, he thought. I've got *math* problems as well.

It was nearly suppertime before Aunt Mary finally released her reluctant pupil. Indy set out immediately to find Lizzie.

Stanzi Rademacher, however, hadn't seen her since lunch. Nor had Indy's father. "Maybe she went off on an outing with that Halani fellow," the professor suggested.

Indy pushed down a surge of jealousy and searched for Mike. But the Hawaiian was nowhere around Volcano House, either.

I have a bad feeling about this, Indy thought. He headed for Pilkington's room. The British agent sat up, pillows piled around him. His color was back and he seemed comfortable enough, considering his broken leg.

"Mr. Jones," he said pleasantly. "I was hoping you'd reconsider my request."

"Reconsider, nothing! Tell me what you've gotten Lizzie Ravenall up to." Indy glared at him from the foot of the bed.

"I don't know what you mean." The spy's face was bland as he looked up at Indy. "Miss Ravenall has nursed me. She brought up a tray for lunch."

"Right," Indy said. "And she didn't bring up the secret message she intercepted? Don't play games with me, Pilkington. I know about it. Like an idiot, I helped decode part of it for her."

"I thought it was rather bright, that bit about the *Ostwind*," Pilkington said.

"So what did you have her do?" Indy demanded.

"Why, nothing, my boy," Pilkington replied with a smile.

Uh-huh, Indy thought. I'm no use to him now, so he treats me like a kid, sending me off. Hot anger fought the cold bubble of fear and worry in Indy's stomach. How could he make Pilkington tell him where Lizzie was?

Indy turned away, thinking. So, Pilkington thinks I'm just a kid, does he? Then that's what I'll be. Indy noticed a plate of crackers on the side table, just out of Pilkington's reach.

"Would you like some crackers, sir?" Indy asked in his best little-boy voice. Before Pilkington could answer, Indy picked up the plate, pretended to trip, and dumped cracker crumbs in the Englishman's lap.

"Look what you've done!" Pilkington exclaimed in annoyance.

Indy knew exactly what he'd done. For a man trapped in bed, sitting in itchy cracker crumbs would be torture.

"Since there's no one here, I guess I'll have to help you clean up." Indy kept the same innocent little-boy tone of voice as he went to the washstand.

"Mind what you're doing with that pitcher!" Pilkington cried as Indy stumbled up with a heavy water jug and bowl.

"Eeeyow!" The jug swung within inches of Pilkington's injured leg. "Why don't you go find Miss Ravenall?" The Englishman was almost babbling. "I just asked her to keep an eye on that Messer fellow."

A chill went down Indy's back. "What was she supposed to do if Messer left?"

Pilkington's eyebrows rose in surprise. "Why, I'd expect she'd come and tell me."

Indy set the jug back on the washstand with a clatter. "But you don't know Lizzie," he said, rushing out.

A worried Aunt Mary stood in the lobby as Indy came down the stairs. "Henry," she asked, "have you seen Lizzie around?"

"I think she may have gone out," Indy said cautiously.

"Oh, dear." Aunt Mary's hands began twining together in agitation. "She's gone off on one of her adventures again, hasn't she? Lizzie is a delightful girl, but quite... headstrong, I'm afraid. Since she got friendly with that Mike Halani, she's often"—she looked unhappily at Indy—"given me the slip."

"Don't worry, Aunt Mary, I'll track them down," Indy promised. "If we're not back in time for supper, you can tell everyone the three of us went out."

"Good idea," Aunt Mary said.

And better for me, Indy thought. Now I have permission to go after them. Indy headed for the hotel stables. Several stalls were empty.

A young stable boy was pitchforking dirty

hay into a wheelbarrow. He stopped when he saw Indy. "Yes, sir?"

"I see some people have gone riding," Indy said.

The boy got shifty-eyed. "I wouldn't know." He turned back to his work.

Indy jingled some coins in his pocket. The boy glanced back.

"The German gentleman left first, right?" Indy said. "Did he mention which way he was going?"

"He gave me a quarter not to tell," the stable boy said bluntly.

Indy pulled a quarter from his pocket. The stable boy frowned. "That blond girl gave me fifty cents."

Trust Lizzie to raise the price, Indy thought as he pulled out another quarter. "She rode off after him, right?"

The boy nodded. "With her Hawaiian friend. Straight for Hilo."

Indy pulled more coins from his pocket. "I need a horse, too," he said. "The fastest you've got."

The stable boy shrugged. "The fastest I've got left," he said.

At least it's a downhill chase, Indy thought. He pushed his horse as fast as he dared, considering the state of the road. But by the time he reached Hilo, he still hadn't caught up with Lizzie and Mike.

Indy picked up their trail at a livery stable where he left his horse. A quarter to that stable boy got the news that they'd headed for the harbor.

A group of Hawaiian fishermen were cleaning their nets as Indy came up. "Did you see a blond man down here? Thick?" He put his hands out to either side of his body and imitated Messer's bull-like walk.

A fisherman chuckled: "Yellow-hair *haole* come by while ago. Get on big ship."

Indy sighed with relief. That's that, he thought. Good, Lizzie couldn't follow any farther.

"You second one to ask," said another fisherman. "*Haole wahine* come, too."

A *wahine*—a girl. That had to be Lizzie, Indy thought.

"What did she say?" he asked.

"Angry when she hear man sail away," a third fisherman put in. "Angrier when she hear no boats left to rent. So she and a friend buy surfing boards. They go off that way. Same way as ship." He pointed out toward the horizon.

Oh, *no*! Indy thought in dismay. But he kept a calm face. "Where can I get a surfing board?" he asked.

"Only one left belongs to my son," the first fisherman said. "May be too little for you."

The board was shorter than any Indy had seen—only seven feet tall. The taller ones would go faster, but beggars couldn't be choosers. "How much?" he asked.

"Ten dollar," the fisherman said.

Indy checked his pockets. "I've only got three dollars and eighty-two cents."

The fisherman shook his head. "Son's board." Then he glanced at Indy's feet. "Nice shoes."

"What?" Indy couldn't believe this.

"Might trade for the shoes."

Rolling his eyes, Indy hopped to the board as he removed his shoes. The fisherman got the money, too.

Indy launched into the surf before he bargained anything else away. He headed in the direction the fisherman had indicated. Oh, well, he thought as he paddled through the harbor. The last thing I need out here is shoes.

What I do need, he realized as he fell off, is more surf-riding lessons. Just paddling his way through the breakers was hard enough. Indy swam for the board and finally managed to crawl back on. It took several tries till, with wobbly knees, he managed to stand on it.

Indy's plan was to stand on the board and scan the horizon for Lizzie and Mike. Once he spotted them he would get back down on the board and paddle his way out to them. But no sooner did he stand up than he toppled back in the water. And the same thing happened time after time, until finally he gave up.

Great—I lost my shoes for nothing! thought Indy. He tried to head the board back to shore. But the harder he paddled with his arms, the more the land seemed to recede.

Suddenly he felt the water pulling him

from below. Oh, great, he thought, the current is pulling me out. I set off to rescue Lizzie, and I get myself in trouble! He paddled till his shoulders ached, but the current swept him ever farther out to sea. And there were no other surfers or boats all the way to the horizon.

With Hilo long out of sight, Indy began realizing he could die at sea. There were so many ways—starvation, thirst... Or just plain exhaustion could make him fall off the board and drown.

Indy scanned the empty sea with growing fear. Not only was the sun starting to set, but in the distance he saw a large dark cloud.

Oh, perfect, a storm, he thought. That was one thing he hadn't thought of.

Then a dot appeared on the horizon beneath the cloud. It was a steamship, traveling under a plume of smoke!

As the ship came nearer, Indy saw that it was an old-fashioned freighter. It even had two masts like the *China Maid*.

But this ship flew the Norwegian flag.

Indy could feel his heart beating hard. If

they pick me up, I'm saved! he thought.

Carefully, he stood up on the surfing board. "Ahoy!" he yelled, waving his arms.

The ship chugged on.

They can't hear me, Indy thought. But they're heading this way. Frantically, he unbuttoned his shirt, tore it from his body, and began waving it.

"Hey!" he cried. "Man overboard."

The ship was much closer now. Surely they could hear him. But the ship just kept sailing on.

A sailor on the *China Maid* had come from Norway, and Indy had picked up a few words. Desperately, he screamed the Norwegian word for help. "*Hjelpe!*"

His voice was lost in the throbbing of steam engines. Indy stared up at the prow as it suddenly loomed over him. He dropped to his knees and began paddling frantically. The stupid ship was going to run him down!

Chapter 10

The wake of the ship speeding past him swamped Indy's little board. His wet shirt slapped him in the face, and for a moment he was blinded. He quickly clawed the shirt aside, threw it away, and struggled through turbulent water to grab hold of the board.

His head popped above the surface and he gasped for breath. High above, he heard a voice crying in a foreign language, "All engines stop!"

Then, "Man overboard!"

Indy was too busy spitting up seawater to hear any more.

The crew was well trained. In seconds, the dinghy was dropped into the water. It came winging toward Indy. The sailors, he noticed, rowed with military precision.

Only as Indy and his board were hauled onto the boat did he realize that the order to stop, and the distress cry, hadn't been in Norwegian. Indy knew enough to tell the difference. He'd spent time in Austria as a child. Whoever had given those orders had spoken in German.

Indy's mind whirled as he glanced from the Norwegian flag to the young men around him. They wore all kinds of clothing. But all of them had their hair cropped short—to a military length.

Indy forced his lips to move. "Thanks for the rescue. You really saved my bacon."

"Excuse?" one of the sailors said.

"Do you speak English?" Indy asked.

"A little," the sailor said.

A voice speaking German broke in. "Find out what he was doing out here," the petty officer steering the boat commanded.

The sailor tried. "What you do here?"

"Surf-riding." Indy pointed to the board. "You stand on this to ride on waves. But the tide went out, and I was caught."

On hearing the sailor's translation, the

petty officer shook his head. "Idiot Americans," he muttered in German.

"What are we going to do with him?" the young sailor asked.

The petty officer merely shrugged. "That's up to wiser heads than ours."

The boat was winched up, and Indy was turned over to a thickset older man with a gray mustache and a jolly smile. He looked like everybody's uncle—except for the sharp eyes.

This must be the wiser head they spoke of, Indy thought. He looks like some sort of bosun's mate.

The officer smiled at Indy. "Welcome aboard the *Nora*," he said in excellent English. "My name is Thorvald. You are...?"

"Henry Jones," Indy replied. "I was surf-riding out at Hilo—I don't suppose you're going there?"

"I'm afraid not," Thorvald said. "Young Ingmar told me your story." He sighed. "I don't know where we can put you ashore."

"Anywhere would be just fine," Indy said. "I'd hate to get my family all worried."

If they think the Coast Guard will come

looking, they'll want to get rid of me, Indy thought. As he looked at Thorvald, he suddenly hoped "getting rid of" would mean putting him on land.

"This is a very nice ship," Indy babbled on. He tried to sound innocent. "Everything looks so fresh and new."

In fact, except for the fresh paint job, the steamship looked amazingly like the *China Maid*. But then, Indy thought, most small old steamers probably looked alike.

"Just what we need," one of the sailors muttered from behind. "He's probably bad luck."

"Yes, but *he* has *good* luck," another sailor said in German. "What if Messer were here instead of running the raid at Hilo? He'd probably have run the American down." Indy had to hide his shock at hearing Messer's name. It certainly sounded like the Messer he knew. But what was this about a raid at Hilo?

Apparently, Indy didn't hide his shock well enough. *"Sprechen sie Deutsch?"* Thorvald suddenly asked.

Indy turned a carefully blank face to the

bosun's question as to whether he spoke German. "Huh?"

"I was just asking if you spoke Norwegian," Thorvald said carelessly.

"Just English, I'm afraid," Indy said. "And now a little Hawaiian. Do you know the word *aloha* means both 'hello' and 'good-bye?'"

"Really?" Thorvald said, then glanced behind Indy and yelled, "Watch your head!"

Instinctively, Indy ducked. And too late, he realized the warning had come in German. He found himself looking down the barrel of a Luger pistol.

"It seems you were too modest about your knowledge of German," Thorvald said.

No, I wasn't, Indy thought. I don't know the German for "Aw, nuts!"

Thorvald marched Indy up to the wheelhouse, where a tall, thin man stood, dressed in a double-breasted blue frock coat. It was the uniform of a German naval captain. The captain had a thin, aristocratic face and a neatly trimmed beard. He looked at Indy in dismay.

"Sorry, sir," Thorvald said. "But he knows

German and began acting suspiciously."

The captain gave Indy a stiff bow. "Kapitan zur See Heinrich Schlageter, commander of the auxiliary cruiser *Ostwind*."

"This is a warship?" Indy said in disbelief. "It looks like a civilian vessel."

"It was," Schlageter admitted, "until we made some changes. Our navy is heavily outnumbered. We need more ships. I am forced to use disguise to pursue enemy trading vessels."

Several seamen were working on a large crate set on the foredeck. Suddenly, Indy heard a loud twang, like a spring breaking. The sides of the crate fell away and revealed a cannon hidden inside.

"Himmel!" Thorvald swore as he rushed up to yell at the men. "What are you doing? That crate should open only on command!"

"You sail under false colors to raid British trading vessels?" Indy asked.

Schlageter looked uncomfortable. "I would prefer a real fighting ship under my feet, but that is not possible. So I fight for the Fatherland where I can—even if it means trying out strange new ways of war."

"I can't believe you came all the way from Germany in this," Indy said.

"Our crew comes from naval ships based in China," Schlageter said. I served under Kapitan von Muller of the *Emden*."

Indy nodded. "I've heard of the *Emden*."

Schlageter smiled with pride. "This ship was originally Russian. It was the first to be captured by the *Emden*. We were quickly refitted and sent out from our German port at Tsingtao, China." The captain frowned. "Unfortunately, we had little coal and less ammunition. I set sail for Hawaii in hopes of obtaining both."

"But America is neutral," Indy said. "You'd just end up interned, like the other German ships in Honolulu harbor."

"We pretended to be an American ship, the *China Maid*, and loaded ourselves with coal." Schlageter looked embarrassed again. "It was a ruse of war," he explained.

"Oh, yeah?" Indy asked. "I was on the real *China Maid*. Was it a ruse of war when one of your people planted a dynamite bomb on board?"

"What?" Schlageter turned shocked eyes

on Indy. "That was not the plan! Messer assured me that the American ship would merely be delayed."

"*Permanently* delayed," Indy said. "What's he up to now?"

Schlageter's face stiffened. "Nothing that concerns you," he said. "We will be out of American waters by tonight."

"It *is* my concern," Indy replied. "A British agent is on Messer's trail, and he's gotten two of my friends to follow him."

The worries that Indy had been holding in flooded through him now. What had happened to Lizzie and Mike?

"You didn't pick up any other Americans, did you?" Indy asked.

Schlageter shook his head. "Only you have seen us. And that is problem enough."

"Oh, right," Indy said. "So, what are you going to do with me? One of the sailors said that if Messer were in charge, you'd just have run me down."

"Indeed not!" Schlageter said, with an uneasy look on his face. "That would not be proper."

Indy looked at the German captain. He was probably a good and careful officer, just what a peacetime navy needed. But this war had him scared out of his wits.

Maybe he's the captain, but he's not running this ship, Indy suddenly realized. Messer is.

"Where are you taking me?" he finally asked.

"We sail for the southwestern coast, near the volcano Kilauea," Schlageter replied. "The land is uninhabited."

That's the area Pilkington wanted to check last night, Indy thought. So the spy had been right. And if he had spotted this ship, British cruisers would be hunting the *Ostwind,* no matter what flag it flew.

"There is a small cove nearby," continued the captain. "We shall anchor beyond the reefs, then meet with Messer and his comrades."

And decide what to do with me, Indy added silently.

The throb of the *Ostwind*'s engines stopped. On the beach in the distance, Indy could see a bonfire. Captain Schlageter turned him over to Thorvald, who marched him back to the dinghy.

As the bosun took the boat's tiller, Indy listened to the griping of the crew.

"Messer took a big chance, stealing the ammunition from the Americans," one man said nervously. "Why did he unload it? He's a sitting duck on that beach."

"You're right," another sailor said. "It would have been easier if he'd stayed on his boat. He could have met us at sea, and we could have taken the crates aboard."

"But what if ships from the naval base came searching for Messer's boat?" Thorvald grumbled. "Better to hide on the beach in darkness. I'm sure Messer didn't light the signal fire until he knew it was the *Ostwind* sailing by."

"*Ja,*" a third crew member said glumly. "But now we must row through those reefs."

Captain Schlageter stepped aboard, and Thorvald launched the dinghy. As the crew rowed to shore, Indy could just make out the reefs. They looked like streaks of white foam in the surf. Getting past them was like riding a zigzag roller coaster.

At last, the group reached the beach. Messer waited with a crew of armed men. Well away from the fire was a pile of crates, marked in red, DANGER! EXPLOSIVES!

And standing by the fire were two bedraggled figures: Lizzie and Mike.

Chapter 11

Lizzie was astonished to find a familiar face among those disembarking from the dinghy.

"Indy!" she burst out. "What are you doing here?"

"I came to rescue you." Indy gave her a lopsided grin. "But things didn't exactly work out that way." He nodded at the Luger Thorvald held on him.

Messer was not pleased with Indy's arrival. *"Ach!"* he growled. "Another blasted American. I found these two following me on those foolish Hawaiian boards. How many more will we manage to collect before we finish here? Will your father appear from a submarine? Or perhaps your aunt will visit us in a flying machine?"

"They are noncombatants," Schlageter said nervously. He stepped through the surf. "Under the rules of war, we must—"

Messer interrupted the peacetime sailor. "In a war, there is only one thing we *must* do, Herr Kapitan. We must survive. Otherwise, we cannot win."

The lieutenant lowered his bull-like head. Every muscle was held stiffly. "We dare not let these two and their native servant free. They will alert the authorities. And the American navy has ships at Hilo that can move much faster than our *Ostwind*."

"We could intern them at one of our colonies," Schlageter suggested.

Even Indy stared at the captain. It seemed as if Schlageter had no idea what was happening in this war.

Messer struggled to keep himself under control. "Sir," he finally said, "I doubt we have any Pacific colonies *left*. The British and Australians are attacking, and the Japanese lust after our land. Interning these people is out of the question."

"Then we shall sail on and leave them in

some neutral port." Schlageter tried to tuck a trembling hand into his coat.

"Where they will reveal to the world that we broke the rules of war," Messer said heavily. "We have already violated American neutrality, defrauded an American ship of coal, and stolen cannon balls. Not honorable deeds, Herr Kapitan, but necessary for the Fatherland."

Captain Schlageter seemed to age years before their very eyes. "And what would you do about these poor people?" His voice was almost a whisper.

"They will have an accident," Messer said bluntly. "A fatal accident."

"B-but they are innocent—"

"They involved themselves in a war," Messer said harshly. "People die in wars— and some of the dead are far more innocent than these. What about the civilians who live in the Belgian cities our armies are shelling? Their only sin is living on land our armies must pass through. But this willful girl and foolish boy, not to mention the oafish native—they threaten us by their very existence."

Messer's eyes burned as he stared at his superior officer. "Thus, sir, with the greatest respect—"

He doesn't sound too respectful, thought Indy.

"—I recommend that they cease to exist."

The captain turned a bloodless face away. Gone was the officer so proud of his navy. Instead, Indy saw a stooped old man with lost eyes. Heinrich Schlageter had seen the face of war—and it had broken him. "Remove the prisoners," he said in a dead voice.

"And?" Messer pressed.

The suddenly shrunken captain stared into the flames. "I leave their fate to your discretion, Leutnant Messer," he whispered.

It wasn't a direct order, but Messer had what he wanted. He turned to Thorvald. "I'll need two men—make sure they're armed with rifles. We'll dispose of the Americans." He pointed to the crates of artillery shells on the beach. "You make sure those get aboard the *Ostwind*," he said.

"W—what are you going to do to us?" Lizzie was pale, but she somehow managed to keep her voice steady.

"It is as I just told my captain, Fräulein," Messer answered. "It is quite simple. You will suffer a fatal accident. The Ring of Craters—with the road that swine Pilkington asked about—is above us. We will march up the slope of the volcano until we find a good hole for you to fall into."

Messer frowned in his methodical way. "Perhaps we should leave traces of your presence nearby—clues to make searchers think you were lost in some mishap."

"That won't work," Indy said. "People know we were following you."

"Ah, but I will be disappearing, too— although in a different way. Perhaps I'll leave a hint that I died with you." He nodded to Lizzie. "It seems, Fräulein, I may need my jacket back."

Indy had been so happy to see Lizzie alive, he hadn't noticed how oddly she was dressed. Now he realized she looked like a ragamuffin. She was wearing a pair of floppy sailor's trousers and Messer's blue lieutenant's jacket.

"Lizzie," Indy said, "what happened?"

"I, um, needed a change of clothes when they caught me." For a second, Lizzie looked embarrassed; then she said defiantly, "*You* try staying on one of those boards in a skirt, without it getting soaking wet!"

They stared at each other and almost burst into laughter. But at that moment a pair of sailors arrived, rifles at the ready. A fat-faced seaman poked Indy with his weapon. "*Schnell!*" he ordered.

Indy was tempted to grab the gun when a hand landed on his shoulder. "Don't," Mike Halani warned in a pain-filled voice. "I tried it."

Seeing the young Hawaiian man's features close up, Indy realized that Mike had taken a severe beating. He had a black eye that was puffed nearly shut, and a bruise that continued down his cheek. His lips were split and swollen. And besides all that, there were innumerable welts and black-and-blue marks on his body. Indy didn't know how Mike could stay on his feet.

"The native was foolish enough to try resistance," Messer said, drawing a Luger. "Now, march."

As they started up the mountainside, mist began blowing in from the ocean. Wisps and streamers of fog twisted around them as they climbed. Down the slope, the beach bonfire became a murky glow. Ahead, vague orange spots of shimmering light revealed the location of lava pits.

Indy paid attention only to the rocky terrain under his bare feet. The lava had dried into *pahoehoe*, the wrinkled, ropy stone. At least our soles won't be cut up as we climb, Indy thought.

Suddenly the desolate expanse of bare stone was broken by a thicket of bushes, with soft ferns underfoot. Indy recognized the red berries.

Mike's bruised lips twitched in a painful smile. "*Ohelo* bushes are always the first to come back on the lava flows," he said.

He glanced at Indy. "I should never have let Lizzie talk me into this," he confessed.

Indy could only shrug. "Sounds familiar. I've said the same words to myself many times. Who'd have guessed we'd all wind up as sacrifices to Pele?"

His voice faltered as the wisps of fog

seemed for a second to congeal into a female figure pointing toward the bushes.

Mike had been looking down. But it seemed that Lizzie had noticed. She turned toward the bushes with an expression of wild hope on her face.

Indy knew that look. On other, earlier adventures they'd had weird encounters not easily explained by science. Well, Indy thought, we'll *need* magic to get us out of this fix.

Lizzie halted, and quickly stripped berries off the branches. She'd collected a double handful before one of the guards came up. It was the young man who'd originally questioned Indy when he'd been pulled onto the boat.

"No! Stop!" he cried. He brought his rifle up.

But Lizzie glared back defiantly. "What are you going to do?" she demanded. "Shoot me? Fine. Then you'll have to carry me all the way up."

The German scowled, looking baffled. Lizzie turned around and flounced ahead.

Messer marched them to the nearest vent

hole in the side of the volcano. A dull orange glow reflected off the cloud of smoke pouring from it. The air grew warmer with every step they took. Soon they were almost at the lip of the miniature crater.

"Let us think about the evidence," Messer said. "Jones, perhaps you could leave your wallet."

"It's completely waterlogged," Indy said as he took his wallet out and clutched it.

"I should think this heat would dry it," the German replied. "And, Fräulein, that is a lovely brooch on your blouse."

"It was my mother's." Lizzie looked down at the berries in her hands. "Mike, could you take it off?" she said.

Silently, Mike removed the brooch and handed it to Messer.

Messer briefly looked the young Hawaiian man over. "I don't think we'll need any evidence from you," he said. "Walk forward, and off the edge." He gestured with his Luger. "Fräulein, my jacket, if you please."

"Wait a second!" Lizzie confronted the German, her face pale. "Don't we get a moment, for—for a prayer?"

"A last request?" Messer scoffed.

Indy figured it was a waste of time to appeal to the German's mercy. He aimed instead for Messer's sense of order. "It *is* customary," Indy said.

"*Ach.*" Messer suddenly looked serious. "Very well. We shall allow one prayer."

Lizzie tossed both handfuls of berries into the fiery interior of the vent. "Pele!" she cried. "If that was you I helped last night, please help me now!"

Indy felt the gun at his back. What help will we get from a prayer to a heathen goddess? he thought.

But suddenly there was no time for thinking. The whole mountain rumbled. Mike, Indy, Lizzie, and their captors stumbled back as steam shot from the craterlet where they stood.

And hundreds of feet above them, from the fire pit of Halemaumau, home of Pele, molten lava jetted up more than a thousand feet into the night sky!

Chapter 12

The solid ground heaved under them. The volcano was like a huge animal trying to buck them off. But the display was so spectacular that they could not keep their eyes off it, even while struggling to keep their balance.

Indy snapped back to the real world before the others did. He whirled on one of the guards, the fat one, and managed to plant his fist right in the man's nose. The sailor went down cold.

"Lizzie! Mike! Run for it!" Indy yelled.

The younger guard was too far away for Indy to jump him as well. But the sailor stood frozen, literally too frightened to move, as the mountainside convulsed under his feet.

Mike and Lizzie saw their chance and dashed away. Indy started after them. But the mountain leaped again and sent him into a stumble that spun him right around.

Higher up the slope he saw Kurt Messer aim his Luger at the fleeing pair. Indy had to stop him, but with what? All he had was his wallet, still clutched tightly in his hand.

Instinctively, Indy flung the wallet like a baseball, catching Messer in the side of the face. The German jumped. And his shot went high. Without looking back, Lizzie and Mike sped farther down the mountainside.

The ground shuddered again, and an awful belching noise filled the air. It was like the sound of a bubble making its way through the thickest oatmeal of all time. Indy, Messer, and the young sailor glanced around. Lava had begun to well up from cracks higher on the side of the mountain.

Rivulets of red-hot stone flowed as fast as water down the higher, steeper reaches of the volcano. Indy lunged into a mad dash.

German bullets seemed a small danger compared with the threat of being burned to death.

The ridged surface of the rock underfoot now became cruel on Indy's bare feet. He ran as fast as he could, turning to his left, away from Lizzie and Mike's escape route. Give the Germans different targets, he thought. That way they'll have to split their fire.

But the Germans had shoes, which made pursuit easier. The young sailor made a dash for Indy. But even he cried out when he tried to cross a patch of sharp, pointy *aa* lava. Keen edges of upward-jutting rock sliced through his stout soles. Although he was almost on top of Indy by now, he hopped to a halt. And he yelled in fear.

Lava came spurting down a dried streambed only yards to their left. A blast of heat struck them like a physical blow. Smoke rose from the orange-yellow rock, which churned fiercely. Dark spots appeared in the gurgling brook as bits of lava congealed. The sailor scrambled away from it.

Indy had to retreat, too. It was bad

enough losing ground trying to avoid the sharp field. But now the lava flow cut off his escape. He'd have to head to the right again. It was as if some force—could it be Pele?—was pushing him back in the direction of his friends. Unfortunately, he'd meet the oncoming Germans first.

But as Indy came toward the Germans, he discovered they had problems, too. The fat guard had woken up and staggered to his feet, but he had lost time and gotten trapped on the upper slope. A stream of lava cut him off. Now a broad flow of burning stuff advanced steadily from behind him. And to make matters worse, his gun was gone. Wailing pitifully, he crouched on an ever-shrinking island of untouched rock.

Messer had obviously given up on the fat man. So he himself took potshots at Lizzie and Mike. The rest of the time, he screamed orders at the young sailor to fire at the two escapees.

The lava following the streambed spurted around in a glowing curve. It began to cut between the Germans and the two fugitives, raising a curtain of smoke and shimmering air. Soon the burning stone reached the stand of bushes where Lizzie had picked the *ohelo* berries.

Under Messer's screaming orders, the young sailor finally stopped and aimed. At the same moment, the lava writhed out of the creek bed and into the berry patch.

Instantly, at the merest touch of lava, the bushes burst into flame. The little thicket became a raging inferno. Thick white smoke billowed from the charred shrubs, momentarily hiding Lizzie and her Hawaiian friend.

Lava had saved Indy's friends. But now it followed them. Still worse, the molten stone had trapped Indy. There was only one way around the lava flow—and that way led right past Messer and the young sailor.

The young rifleman was about ten feet to Indy's right. He'd given up trying to aim downhill at Lizzie and Mike. Instead, he kept casting anxious glances backward, toward the lava that had already buried his fat friend. Just as Indy drew near, the young man finally lost his nerve. He threw down his rifle and began running away.

Messer shrieked in fury. As Indy came

closer, he saw the German twist around, aim his pistol...

Indy's skin tightened. He expected the bullet to pierce him any second now. The Luger blasted, and Indy stumbled. But there was no pain. How could Messer have missed?

Then Indy heard a choking cry to his left. The young seaman was down. It was not Indy whom Messer had shot at. It was one of his own men. The sailor had been executed for being a deserter, Indy realized.

That left just Messer in pursuit, Indy thought. But then there was no time for thinking. An enormous *KA-BOOM!* nearly deafened Indy and Messer. The heaving mountain threw both of them to their knees. Indy staggered to his feet and ran past the German. Glancing over his shoulder, he saw Messer crawling uphill.

You're going the wrong way, Indy thought.

Indy's ears caught a high-pitched whistling sound. Then came a crash like an exploding artillery shell, as a red-hot boulder smashed into the ground.

Indy paid no attention to the blast. He

ran to his right, trying to circle around the lava and rejoin his friends.

The air stank of sulfur and seemed full of cinders. Indy's throat burned as he tried to suck air into his aching lungs.

Then from behind, he heard Messer cry, "Jones!"

Indy whirled. The German was staggering to his feet with a rifle in his hands—the gun the young sailor had abandoned. Messer looked like a demon just escaped from hell. He was only a silhouette, a black smudge against the spraying fountains of blinding-hot lava.

And with the rifle in his hands, Messer was as deadly as the scorching rock.

"First you, Jones," he promised grimly. "Then your friends there down the slope. They're still in range."

Indy stood helpless as a bug on a table. The ridges of *pahoehoe* couldn't hide him, and the bare rock provided no weapons.

But raising his fists, he charged up the slope of the volcano. It was hopeless, he knew. Bare hands could never win against a rifle.

Before he'd taken three steps, the mountain jolted again. This was the hardest tremor yet. It flung Indy against the rock. Messer was knocked down, as well.

Beyond the German, what looked like a fireworks display blasted from the summit of Kilauea crater. Blazing white stars launched into the air around the sky-high orange fountain.

Indy struggled up on all fours. A thin whistling sound pierced the air as some of the lava returned to earth. A clump of cooling stone dropped like a shooting star. This was the closest one yet.

Messer pushed himself onto his knees. The rifle was still in one hand. Wobbling slightly, he brought the gun up.

"Messer!" Indy called. He pointed upward. "Look out!"

"You can't fool me with that childish trick, American." Messer's voice was harsh as he aimed the rifle.

With the way that my luck has been running, Indy thought, Messer won't get hit until *after* he shoots me.

All the same, Indy hurled himself to the

side as Messer's gun went off.

The *crack* of the rifle was lost in a thunderous roar. A huge half-molten boulder crashed down where Messer was standing. Indy caught a bare glimpse as Messer was hit. At the same moment he felt the rifle's bullet whiz past his ear.

Indy rose and began running again.

And he didn't look back.

The slope was less steep here, so the lava ran slower. But more bomblike rocks dropped from the sky. Indy felt as if he were racing through an artillery barrage.

Yet another tremor jarred him to the ground. The roar of flying stone filled his ears. As Indy got to his feet, he saw a huge fissure appear about halfway up the mountainside. A broad, fast-spreading flow of lava spilled out.

One look gave Indy the bad news. He'd never get around the old lava flow before the new lava caught up to him. That left only one choice. He'd have to get *across* the old lava—and quick.

Taking a deep gulp of nearly unbreathable air, Indy ran for a narrow place in the lava-filled streambed. As he threw himself into a wild broad jump, he heard the hiss of molten stone oozing downhill. Heat scorched him as if he'd leaped over a furnace. But then he felt cooler air. He landed on the rock on the far side of the creek bed.

More lava gushed down. It created a monstrous river of fire. Flames filled the air over the lava stream.

One second later, and I'd have been cooked in midair, Indy thought.

He lurched to his feet and stumbled down the slope.

"Indy! Over here!" A voice came out of the sooty darkness. It was Lizzie!

She and Mike stood on the side of a small rise ending as a cliff overhanging the sea. Indy glanced up the mountainside. The new lava flowing from the fissure had painted a wide area of the slope a ghastly glowing orange. Still worse, the lava seemed headed straight for them.

Indy forced his bruised feet into a new race against the burning rock. Mike and Lizzie hauled him up the hillock just moments before the surging lava began lapping around the base of the small rise.

"Come on!" Lizzie urged between coughs.

The lava level kept rising. Still worse, it was flowing past either side of their little hill, right into the sea.

Choking steam rose from the water as orange liquid turned to blackish solid. The lava crust kept cracking with a sound like gunshots as more molten stone burst out.

"We'll have to swim for it," Mike said worriedly, "and quick. Soon that water will be hot enough to boil us."

Lizzie rubbed a hand across her face, smearing cinders. "I wasn't leaving without you, Indy."

"Let's dive," Indy said, hoping his friends hadn't waited too long.

They lined up over the deepest water. "Do you know what you're doing?" Mike asked.

"No," Indy admitted. "But we don't have much choice." He glanced at the rising tide of fiery rock behind them.

Aiming as far from the lava as possible, they hurled themselves into the sea.

Chapter 13

Indy was tired. He hurt all over. And even if he'd been in excellent shape, he wasn't great at diving. But something happened that would have thrown off even the best diver.

The lava stream threatening their little hill flowed farther down the coast. It reached the beach where the *Ostwind*'s boat had landed. Indy was in mid-dive, high in the air, when he saw the crates abandoned by the shore. The artillery shells were still down there!

The lava rolled over the cases, and the beach disappeared in a series of explosions. Perhaps they weren't as impressive as what the volcano had come up with. But they were enough to distract Indy. Even then, he might have been all right except for the huge explosion out at sea.

It happened an instant before he hit the water. One second, he was managing a graceless but decent enough dive. The next, he was deafened—and landing in a belly flop.

Indy sank through the water, stunned, for precious seconds. Then he pulled himself together and clawed his way to the surface. Where was Lizzie? Where was Mike?

Indy was so busy searching, he failed to notice that the water was growing dangerously warm.

"Indy! Get out of there!" Lizzie's voice rang sharply in his ear. She swam behind him, slipped an arm around his chest, and kicked off for deeper water.

I wonder if I look as bad as I feel, Indy thought as he let Lizzie help him. Then he saw Mike Halani up ahead. I probably look even worse than I feel, he thought.

Their dip had not washed all the cinders away from Mike's face. The water had just streaked the dirt. At least I don't have bruises, like poor Mike, Indy told himself.

Indy's dulled brain wrestled with a problem. How could he see Mike so clearly? The moon and stars were hidden by smoke from the eruption.

Then he noticed light streaming from beyond the young Hawaiian. It took Indy a moment to recognize that the hulk ablaze on the water had once been the *Ostwind*.

Lizzie stared as her tired limbs beat against the water. "So their stolen shells sank their ship," she said between breaths.

"Could have been Pele." Indy tried to smile against the strain of treading water. "She bombed the cove with rocks."

"But the sea god is Pele's enemy." Mike's voice slurred in exhaustion. "Can't swim all the way back to Hilo."

All three of them had reached the end of their strength. But everywhere within swimming distance was threatened by lava.

Indy realized they had only one choice left. "What are you doing?" Lizzie cried in dismay as he struck farther out, heading for the crippled ship.

Happily, Indy's instinct turned out right. He found a huge, flat piece of wood floating in the water near the wreck. Probably, he thought, it had been a wall from one of the phony crates hiding the *Ostwind*'s guns.

Indy clung to the splintery wood as if it were made of gold. "Over here!" he called to the others. "This will keep us afloat!"

Mike sighed gratefully as he leaned against the makeshift life raft. Lizzie, however, looked across the water and gasped.

"What's that?" she cried out.

Indy made out something cutting through the water toward them. Then he realized it wasn't something, but some*one*.

"You survived!" a familiar voice cried.

It was Captain Schlageter, very much changed. His frock coat was gone, and his white shirt was blackened with smoke. So was most of his skin. Faded blue eyes peered from behind a mask of grime.

Anger gave Indy new strength. He swam to block the captain's path. "Thanks to you, we were thrown around, shot at, and nearly cooked by lava. Go find your own piece of wreckage!"

"Indy, let him stay!" Lizzie cried. "After all," she said, "he's lost his ship."

"My ship?" Schlageter echoed. "That's the least of it. I lost my honor—and my part of the war. It is only fair."

"What happened out there?" Lizzie asked.

"When the volcano began to erupt, I ordered my crew off the beach and back to the ship." Schlageter's voice firmed, as if he were giving a military report. "We couldn't carry anything more on the dinghy, so we left several crates of ammunition behind. Then, as we were raising steam to pull back, the mountain exploded again. Something— a rock?—smashed through the deck. The boiler room was flooded. We couldn't move."

He sighed. "Then the lava came. It reached the shells, and the ship blew up."

Schlageter glanced from the flaming *Ostwind* to the plume of lava soaring from Kilauea. "I do not care for myself, but for my men," he finally said. "My last order was for the crew to escape on the ship's dinghies. I stayed behind and sent off a message on the ship's wireless. Your naval station at Hilo replied."

"Well, isn't that nice of you," Indy growled. "Help is on the way."

Schlageter nodded. "And I and my people will go to prison."

For a second, Indy thought of Messer, who had paid an even higher price for his misdeeds.

"Me, I'm going straight back to Waikiki," Mike suddenly said. His voice broke the mood. "Diamond Head is my kind of volcano—extinct."

"I know what you mean," Lizzie said with a tired laugh. "I'm going back to college. Cracking the books will be adventure enough." Her blue eyes sparkled as they glanced at Indy. "At least for a while."

"So you'll be heading east to New York, and I'll be heading west to China." Indy felt a little stab of disappointment.

"Two ships, passing in the night," Lizzie said lightly.

"I'll miss you, Lizzie. What more can I say?"

"I've got just the word," Lizzie said with a smile. "*Aloha.*"

HISTORICAL NOTE

Hawaii was at one time a country. By 1795, the ruler Kamehameha I had united almost all of the Hawaiian Islands, creating a kingdom that lasted nearly 100 years. The last native ruler was overthrown in 1893 by wealthy American sugarcane planters who, for business reasons, wanted Hawaii to become part of the United States. In 1900 the United States established the Territory of Hawaii, and in 1959 Hawaii became the 50th state in the Union.

All of the Hawaiian locations mentioned in this book, including Volcano House, are actual places. German trading ships did seek the protection of neutral Hawaii at the beginning of World War I, and there was a construction disaster at Pearl Harbor. Work to rebuild the ruined dry dock began in

1915 and was speeded up when America entered the war in 1917. The dock was finished in two years, and Pearl Harbor became an important military base—so important, in fact, that it became the target of a Japanese surprise attack in 1941, which brought the U.S. into World War II.

In the years before World War I, a major sugar operation was owned by a German family (though their name wasn't Rademacher). When the U.S. declared war on Germany, the company was taken over by several competitors and given an "American" name.

Although the *Ostwind* and its plot to refuel and rearm itself are fictional, the German navy did raid Allied merchant ships during World War I. Several raiders disguised as trade vessels terrorized the waves. And the *Emden*, an actual ship, had a brilliant record of hit-and-run warfare until it was sunk.

Kilauea volcano really exists. It is, in fact, a major tourist attraction. Because eruptions are so frequent (and relatively mild), Hawaii is called the land of "drive-in volcanoes."

Major eruptions do occur, however, with great damage to property. Whole towns have disappeared under lava. The eruption in this book is fictional, but it is based on a very violent eruption of Kilauea in 1924. Besides the lava spray, that eruption featured what geologists call "bombs": red-hot boulders that were blown into the air and then fell back to earth. One of these rocks landed on a tourist photographer, who became the first (and so far, only) historical casualty of a Hawaiian eruption.

Whether or not she may be a goddess, Pele is very real to many Hawaiians. She's an *aumakua*, a family god ranked among their ancestors. Pele often appears in legends, sometimes as an old hag, sometimes as a beautiful young woman. All of the stories told about Pele in this book are based on Hawaiian folklore.

The *ohelo* bush is one of the first plants to reestablish themselves on cooled lava. *Ohelo* berries, which are like cranberries, are considered sacred to Pele.

In the 1950s, the air force tried to bomb lava flows to change their direction. Accord-

rumor, at least one pilot, hearing of fondness for strong drink, dropped a bottle of Scotch along with his bombs.

Pele's name has come up more recently in connection with environmental concerns. Fighting a geothermal energy plan to tap power from Hawaii's volcanoes, people formed the Pele Defense Fund.

TO FIND OUT MORE...

Hawaii (America the Beautiful series) by Sylvia McNair. Published by Childrens Press, 1990. This big, full-color illustrated book is a marvelous introduction to the geography, people, and history of Hawaii. Recounts Hawaiian myths and legends, and the intriguing mix of cultures found in the islands. Index.

Volcano & Earthquake (Eyewitness Books). Published by Alfred A. Knopf, 1992. Hundreds of color photographs and drawings help explain what causes these two powerful events. The fascinating section on Hawaii includes photos of highways buried under lava as well as the thin, glassy strands of lava known as "Pele's hair." Index.

Volcano (A Disaster! Book) by Christopher Lampton. Published by Millbrook Press, 1991. This book provides an overview of the causes, types, and locations of volcanoes. Full-color photographs, index, glossary, reading list.

World War I (America at War series) by Peter Bosco. Published by Facts on File, 1991. This book follows the course of the war from 1915 to 1918, concentrating on the United States' involvement and the effects of the war on America. Photos and strategic maps.

The Warship in History by Philip Cowburn. Published by Macmillan, 1965. This book cuts

iers in recounting the role warships
ayed—from ancient vessels to modern
carriers. You won't finish this book in
one night, but if you want to find something
specific, it's here. You can read about the early
submarines that Indy and his dad were worried about as well as the other ships used by
navies in World War I. Check your library for
this one! Photos, index, bibliography.

Ring of Fire (film). Produced and distributed
by the Science Museum of Minnesota, 1991.
This riveting film takes you along as it
explores the volcanoes of the Pacific Rim.
You'll learn what causes volcanoes and see
breathtaking "mountains of fire" in action, just
as Indy did. Footage of Hawaii's active volcanoes is included in the film, which will be
released on video in the fall of 1995.